Needing Nevaeh

ROCKER'S LEGACY

Book Two

USA Today Bestselling Author
TERRI ANNE BROWNING

Copyright © Terri Anne Browning/Anna Henson 2019
All rights reserved. No part of this publication may be reproduced, distributed, or transmitted in any form or by any means, or stored in a database or retrieval system, without the prior written permission of Terri Anne Browning, except as permitted under the U.S. Copyright Act of 1976.

Needing Nevaeh
Rockers' Legacy Book 2
Written by Terri Anne Browning
All Rights Reserved ©Terri Anne Browning 2019
Cover Design Sara Eirew Photography
Edited by Lisa Hollett of Silently Correcting Your Grammar
Formatting by M.L. Pahl of IndieVention Designs

ISBN: 9781708857998

10 9 8 7 6 5 4 3 2 1

Needing Nevaeh is a work of fiction. Names, characters, places, and incidents are the products of the author's imagination or are used fictitiously. Any resemblance to actual events, locales, or persons, living or dead, is entirely coincidental.

No part of this book can be reproduced in any form by electronic or mechanical means, including storage or retrieval systems, without the express permission in writing from the author. The only exception is by a reviewer who may quote short excerpts in a review.

DEMON'S WINGS

EMMIE & NIK
Mia & Barrick
Jagger

JESSIE & LAYLA
Lucy & Harris — Hayat/Evan
Luca
Lyric

DRAKE & LANA
Nevaeh
Arella
Heavenleigh
Bliss
Damien

SHANE & HARPER
Violet
Mason

Needing Nevaeh

ROCKER'S LEGACY

Book Two

Prologue
Nevaeh

I sat staring sightlessly at my computer as Mom picked up the tray still holding the untouched snack she'd brought me earlier. I felt her honey-brown eyes drilling into me, trying to figure out what to say to make last weekend disappear.

My parents were amazing, and I knew if anyone could make what happened even marginally better, they would. But not even they could erase what went down in New York the previous weekend.

At the door, she hesitated. "Nev, I love you. You know that, right?"

I didn't even look away from the computer screen as I whispered, "I know, and I love you too, Mom."

A few moments later, I heard the door click shut behind her, and I closed my eyes. But shutting my eyes only made images of what happened flash in my mind, and I quickly snapped them open, fighting back a fresh wave of tears.

For someone who had an IQ of 178, I'd acted pretty stupid when I'd gone to New York with my grandfather for a charity event. We'd stopped in Northern Virginia to pick up my cousin Mia and her roommate Braxton. I'd been having crazy daydreams about the sexy as hell Brax from the moment I'd seen him during a Skype chat with Mia weeks before, and I'd been just as excited to meet him as I'd been to spend time with my friend.

But from the moment he stepped onto PopPop's private jet, Brax had barely looked at me. My opinion—along with my heart—had only dropped more and more as the evening had worn on, and then Mia had discovered Braxton and her boyfriend had been keeping something huge from her. Mom and I were still a little pissed at Daddy because he'd been a part of the whole scheme, while Mia was so heartbroken, my own heart had ached from her pain.

As Mia had hidden out in her room in the hotel suite where we were staying, I'd spent the time with Braxton. He'd been quiet, brooding, and I actually felt sorry for him. It was obvious he was regretful for his part in keeping Mia in the dark about the fact that he was part of her secret security detail, and for some reason, I couldn't stand the thought of him hurting any more than I could Mia.

But the next day, he left with Mia, going back to Northern Virginia, while I had to stay behind and go to the charity event with PopPop.

All evening, all I could think about was Braxton—and how much I really wanted him to be my first kiss. My first everything.

Not that I expected him to want that too. Hell, I wasn't even sixteen yet, and Braxton wasn't just some boy. He was a man, and I knew he wouldn't be into teaching me all the things I was dying to experience for the first time. Especially not *me*, the awkward girl who freaked out everyone who wasn't family with how I blurted out the oddest and most random things without warning. He'd already shown me he wasn't interested—emphatically. Hell, he could barely even look at me during the little time we'd spent together.

Yet that didn't stop me from fantasizing about it.

How his firm lips would feel against my softer, plumper ones. How he would taste. Where he would touch me—would he pull me hard against him or carefully cup the back of my head? I'd sensed both gentleness and a caged, feral predator in him, and I wanted to experience both sides of Braxton Collins.

I'd been so lost in all the possibilities, I'd drifted away from PopPop without realizing it. And it wasn't until Dax Brightmore, the newest heartthrob in Hollywood and a total tool if ever there was one, spoke to me that I was pulled back into reality. He'd just turned eighteen and already had some major box office movies under his belt, along with the bank account that went with it.

Most girls my age would have no doubt screamed and cried and thrown themselves at Dax as soon as they saw him.

I wasn't most girls.

For one, the whole celebrity thing didn't faze me. My dad was a Demon, and my grandfather was the biggest rock legend in the music industry. I'd been dealing with celebrities of every variety from birth.

For another, I'd already met Dax on several other occasions, and he left a lot to be desired. He was full of himself, high off his popularity—and probably something a hell of a lot stronger from the way his eyes were dilated. Each time I'd met him, he'd tried asking me out, but I wasn't interested.

No one had ever really interested me. Not until Braxton.

Realizing I was alone in a room with Dax had made me nervous, and I didn't understand why until he grabbed me and kissed me.

I'd been so shocked, it had taken a few heartbeats before I'd started to fight him, trying to get away from him. But he was stronger than me, and I couldn't get him to release me.

PopPop saved me, jerking Dax away from me and punching him in the face.

I'd stepped back, scrubbing my hands over my bruised mouth, already crying.

It wasn't a gentle kiss, nor was it full of passion. It was greedy and violent. I didn't feel wanted; I felt violated and ashamed. The taste of his mouth made me want to gag. I could still taste it on my tongue, and it made me shudder every time I licked my lips.

He'd stolen it. My first kiss was taken from me.

I couldn't give it to Braxton or anyone else now.

It was only a kiss; it wasn't like he'd groped me or even tried to rape me. Yet I felt deprived of something special, dirty and used, and I realized no one would ever want to kiss me now.

My phone blaring my ringtone jerked me out of my nightmare. Scrubbing a hand over my wet eyes, I saw it was Mia calling and swallowed the lump that had filled my throat. I didn't want to talk to her—or anyone else—but it was her birthday, so I couldn't just let her go to voice mail.

Picking it up, I walked over to my bed and dropped down onto my stomach before answering. "Happy birthday, Mia!" I greeted as chipperly as I could, given that I was still fighting tears.

"Kitten…" Braxton's voice had me gasping and sitting upright on the edge of my bed, my heart throbbing as a fresh wave of tears flooded down my face. Just the sound of his voice had calmed my anxiety and the nightmare that lived in my head, blocking everything else but what happened, making it disappear for the first time since it took place. "Are you okay?"

I pressed the palm of my free hand into my forehead, wondering if I was hallucinating hearing his voice instead of Mia's. But he'd called me "kitten." Only one person had ever called me that. Braxton.

"Nevaeh?" his deep voice rasped my name when I didn't answer him.

"I-I'm here." I finally found my voice to reply. "Why are you calling me?"

"Mia's mom said something happened last weekend. I just wanted to make sure you are okay." He blew out what sounded like a frustrated sigh. "Are you?"

"Am I what?" I muttered, still trying to wrap my head around the object of my every fantasy actually calling me.

"Okay," he growled. "Are you okay, Kitten?"

"I'm fine," I gritted out, more than a little frustrated myself as the nightmare flooded back into my mind, pushing out everything else. Everyone kept asking if I was okay, and the truth was I didn't know if I was or not. But they all seemed to want to hear that I was fine, so that was what I told them every time.

"Liar," he muttered so quietly, I almost didn't hear him. "Do you… I don't know, maybe you want to talk about what happened?"

I clamped my mouth shut before the words could escape. I wanted to tell him everything, and I didn't understand why. I hadn't told anyone the complete details of the incident. All my parents knew was what PopPop had told them, and even he didn't know the full extent of it. Just that he'd found some guy kissing me and knocked him on his ass.

They didn't know I felt ashamed that I had let some guy even touch me, let alone kiss me. I hated that I couldn't stop him myself, that I was so weak and trapped I couldn't even cry for help. I felt violated and used, and I didn't understand why when a kiss was all he'd taken from me.

And not understanding something just wasn't acceptable to me.

"Mia and Barrick made up, so if you're still up for it, you can move in with us when you come to school out here next semester," he informed me, changing the subject when I remained silent.

That definitely caught my attention. "I'll be living with you?"

Oh shit. How was I going to handle living under the same roof with him when all I wanted was to give him every single one of my other firsts? And despite Dax stealing my first kiss, I still had plenty of other firsts to give away to whomever I wanted.

"Yeah, we were just talking about it at dinner. Mia's parents are on board with it and said they would discuss it with your mom and dad."

"And I'm sure you're thrilled about that," I said with a roll of my eyes, realizing the true reason he was calling. "Look, I'll talk to them and figure something out. You won't even have to see me once I start school."

"What? No," he grumbled. "It was my idea for you to live with us, Kitten. Ask Mia if you don't believe me."

"Maybe I'm the one who should be asking 'are you okay?'" A laugh escaped me, and for a moment, it sounded foreign to my ears because I hadn't laughed in over a week. "You seemed like you couldn't even stand to be around me the other day, Braxton. Why would you want me living under the same roof with you for months at a time?"

"I don't understand it myself, if I'm being honest. But I would feel better about you and Mia living with us than in some apartment with poor security, or in the dorms where who knows what could happen."

"So, this is more about protecting Mia," I said, disappointment hitting me squarely in the chest. "This has nothing to do with me."

"It's not like that," he tried to tell me, frustration thick in his voice. "I want to protect you too."

"It's okay. I get it. You don't have to defend yourself to me." I lay back, picking up the teddy bear I'd slept with most of my life and squeezed him to my chest. "I'm going to get off here. I have some work to do," I lied.

"Nevaeh…" Something in his voice stopped me from hanging up. "If you ever need to talk, you can call me. No matter what time or what it's about, I'll always answer. Okay?"

"I don't have your number," I reminded him.

"I'll text it to you from Mia's phone. I mean it, Kitten. Call me anytime."

"Yeah, okay," I told him, knowing I would never tell him about Dax, but the idea of talking to him whenever I wanted had my lips lifting in the beginning of a smile.

"Call me later." It sounded more like a command than a question, but I still found myself agreeing. "Bye, Kitten."

"Bye, Braxton," I whispered, clenching my arms around the teddy bear.

Chapter 1
Nevaeh

Daddy put the last of my boxes down in the middle of the bedroom that was going to be mine for the foreseeable future, his blue-gray eyes glancing around the average-sized room in the three-bedroom house.

The queen-sized bed was already made up with my favorite comforter and pillows. My laptop sat open on the desk by the window, all the books I needed for the semester course load stacked neatly on the edge. Mom was already putting away my toiletries in the connecting bathroom.

Both of my parents had come with me, making sure I was settled in and didn't need anything. But it was mostly to reassure themselves their sixteen-year-old daughter would be safe and happy three thousand miles away from them. They didn't need to worry, though. Not only was I a reasonably responsible teenager, leaps and bounds away from how immature my younger sister Arella was, but I had Barrick and Braxton to watch over me.

If Uncle Nik could relax and let them take care of Mia, then I knew my parents could handle me being away with those two close by.

"Are you sure you don't need anything else?" Daddy asked as his gaze landed on me. "You have everything for all those classes you're taking?"

"I'm set, Daddy," I said with a grin. Not only had he gone with me to buy all my books, but he'd handed me one of his many limitless credit cards, telling me if I needed—or wanted—anything, not to hesitate to use it. It didn't matter that I had two other cards in my purse. He needed me to take it, and there was nothing I wouldn't do to make him happy.

"If you decide you don't like it here, or if things get to be too much for you, I don't care how far into the semester it is, you come home." He wrapped his arms around my shoulders, cradling me against him like I was still a little girl. I closed my eyes, soaking it all in. I was going to miss him and Mom, but I needed this time away from them and my siblings.

"Okay," I agreed, because he needed me to.

"Don't do anything reckless. No parties. No boys. No drinking and no drugs," he warned.

"Of course, Daddy."

Mom walked out of the bathroom, dusting off her hands like she'd just spent an hour cleaning in there rather than just ten minutes organizing toiletries. Everything in the house was spotless, and I didn't think for a second it was Mia's doing. I loved her like crazy, but she didn't do a lot of cleaning. No, it was the cousins who seemed a little OCD about keeping everything neat and tidy, but that could just as easily be their military background at work.

"Looks like you're all set," she said with a smile. "What do you say we grab some dinner, and then Daddy and I will get out of your hair?"

I lifted my brows at them. "First, you're not in my hair. I love you both and miss you already. Second, you're just looking for an excuse not to leave me. After dinner, you'll talk me into going for ice cream or cheesecake or something equally delicious and fattening. And before you know it, your flight time will be canceled and you will have to wait until morning for a new time for PopPop's jet to get in the air."

Mom looked up at Daddy with sad eyes. "I really don't like that she knows us so well, babe. She's too damn smart for her own good."

"And that is why we're dropping her off at college when she's only just turned sixteen," he grumbled unhappily. "But she's right. We need to go, or I won't want to leave her at all. And we have four other babies at home."

"They're at Shane and Harper's," Mom argued. "They'll be fine a few extra days without us. Our firstborn needs us more, Dray."

"No, I definitely do not need you more than Arella, Heavenleigh, Bliss, or Damien," I assured her.

"Maybe we should rethink the whole distance thing," Daddy told Mom over my head. "I mean, how far was Stanford from our house again? Surely it was a better match for her brain than this school. Or Cal Tech, that would have been perfect. We could even have bought a house close to campus, and she could have stayed home instead of in a dorm."

Rolling my eyes at the same argument they'd tried to pull for the past two weeks, I took each of them by the elbow and steered them to the door. Out to the living room where Aunt Emmie was sitting on the couch with Mia.

"We all agreed this school was a great fit for me. It's smaller, and some of the smartest minds have attended," I reminded them, not for the first time that day.

"Uh oh." I heard Aunt Emmie whisper to Mia. "This is the worst part of all. Be prepared for the waterworks."

On cue, Daddy's eyes flooded with tears. "I'm just worried about you all the way out here all alone. I don't like you being on your own. You're just a baby and—"

"I'm not alone," I told him patiently, my heart aching because I couldn't stand to see my dad sad. "I have Mia. Plus, there are Barrick and Braxton, whom you and the uncles vetted personally, if I remember correctly." His jaw clenched when I reminded him that he and Uncle Nik handpicked Charles Barrick to be Mia's secret security detail. He didn't like thinking of the week he'd spent in the proverbial doghouse with Mom over the whole thing.

"Where are those two anyway?" Mom asked, frowning in Mia's direction. "I want to thank them again for letting Nevaeh stay here before we go."

"They went to do a security consult for a local business," my cousin told her. "I'm not sure when they will be back, but it shouldn't be too much longer. Why don't I order some dinner, and they can pick it up on their way home? Then once we've eaten and you've thanked them—*yet again*—you can get to the airport without missing your takeoff."

While Mia handled my parents like an expert, setting their minds at ease and letting them stay a little longer, I walked over to the couch and took a seat beside Aunt Emmie, who put her arm around my shoulders and gave me a squeeze. "It will be okay," she promised in a whisper only I could hear. "I'll take care of them."

I knew she would help them, but I appreciated her reassurance. My parents weren't weak or unable to take care of themselves. My mom was one of the strongest women I knew, and even though Daddy seemed like a bowl of squishy Jell-O with me and our family, to the outside world, he was viewed with awe for his no-fucks-given attitude and his reputation for tossing paparazzi out windows. He was Drake Fucking Stevenson after all. Revered guitarist for Demon's Wings and one of the biggest badass rockers the world had ever seen.

But he was also an emotional father who was dropping his baby girl off at college for the first time and would spend the next few days mourning my not being in the same house with him and Mom. There were going to be tears and maybe even a few emotional breakdowns in his future, and that was making my heart throb. "Thanks, Aunt Em."

It was almost an hour later before the front door opened and in walked Barrick with a bag of takeout from the local Mexican restaurant. Mia said they had the best tacos, and we were all in agreement that comfort food needed to be on the menu for the evening.

Behind him, carrying a second bag, limped Braxton. He was dressed in black dress pants, a white button-down that molded across his chest, with black combat boots to complete the outfit, and it took me a moment to pull my tongue from the roof of my mouth…because damn. His dark hair was cropped short, his dark eyes hauntingly beautiful with the longest, thickest eyelashes I'd ever seen on a guy. I wanted to spend uninterrupted hours while I just memorized the planes of his face.

How could someone so masculine be so fucking beautiful? It didn't make sense, but the proof was right in front of my eyes and I couldn't pull my gaze from him.

A whine drew my attention away from the Marine vet to see an older German shepherd walking slowly behind him. There was gray in her fur, and she moved like her entire body hurt. From the many phone conversations I'd had with Braxton in the last several months, I knew her name was Sasha and she was seventeen. I knew a lot about the dog, had even fallen in love with her just from the stories he'd told me about her.

But upon seeing her in person, I felt my heart instantly leap, and I found myself greeting her like an old friend. "Hello, sweet puppy," I murmured as I crouched down in front of her, letting her sniff my hand.

I was rewarded with a soft lick to my palm, then one to my chin. I hugged her neck gently, afraid to hurt her. Sasha's tail wagged happily, and she buried her snout in my neck, making me giggle.

"Sasha, easy," Braxton's deep voice commanded, surprising me with its closeness. Lifting my head, I found him standing beside us. Crouching, he smoothed his hand down the dog's back. "She likes you," he murmured. "She's not normally all over people."

"I'm not people," I said, scratching her head. "I'm Sasha's. Right, Sasha baby?" She whined as if agreeing with me, and I laughed. "See? She claimed me."

"That's because Sasha is a smart girl. Aren't you, precious?" he cooed to the dog, stroking her fur.

"Hey, you two," Mia called out. "Food's getting cold. Come eat."

Glancing around, I realized we were the only ones in the living room and Braxton was very, very close. Heat instantly filled my face, and I cleared my throat as I straightened, thankful I wasn't spewing all the things in my head out into reality for him to hear. Like that I wanted him to brush his massive hands down my back like he was Sasha, or that I wanted him to claim me as his just as the dog had.

When he stood, he reached out, stroking the backs of his knuckles down my cheek. "I'm glad you're here," he said with a smile before walking into the kitchen.

I stood there, my heart pounding in my chest, and watched him walk away. "Me too," I whispered, touching my fingers to my cheek where his had made contact.

Chapter 2

It was snowing as I walked across campus. My first class of the day wasn't for another hour, but Mia and Nevaeh each had one that was about to end. Thankfully, they were both in the same building.

"Hey, Braxton," someone called out, and I didn't even look to see who it was. I tossed up my hand in a salute and kept walking.

Opening the door, I walked into a wall of heat, and my muscles started to relax a little as I walked toward Nevaeh's class first. Before I reached the thick, closed door, it opened and students started spilling out.

None of them was my kitten, though.

I waited impatiently for everyone to exit then walked in to find Nevaeh talking to the professor. Arguing was a better word for it.

"Look," she said, frustration heavy in her voice as she waved her hand to the whiteboard where some crazy math equation took up the entire space. "You miscalculated here, and then again here."

"How could you possibly know that just by looking at the equation, Miss Stevenson?" the professor, a man in his late forties, demanded in a tone that suggested Nevaeh couldn't dream of knowing more than him.

"My brain is like a computer when it comes to math," she said with a shrug as if it were no big deal. "I understand mistakes are part of life, but if you can't correct yourself, how will you ever learn?"

"If you know so much, why are you even in this class?" he demanded. "Sounds like you think you already know more than me."

She shrugged. "Probably. But apparently this class is required for my major."

"Miss Stevenson—"

I quickly moved forward when I heard the coldness in his tone. Fuck no, he wasn't going to talk to my little kitten like that. I would knock his damn teeth down his throat before I let him hurt her feelings. "Nevaeh, are you ready?"

She snapped her head around and smiled warmly, seeming to forget about the professor and his mistakes. I glanced at the board again, amusement making my lips twitch that she'd caught this dick in not one, but two mistakes when it looked like a foreign language to me.

"You didn't have to come get me," she said as she walked back to her desk and started packing up her things.

"I want to make sure you get to your next class with no issues," I told her as I picked up her backpack.

She rolled her blue-gray eyes at me, but she couldn't hide the pleasure in them. "You're worse than a new father, you know that? I mean, I'm fairly sure I can read a map if I did happen to get lost."

"I don't doubt that for a second," I assured her with a grin as we left the room and walked toward the exit. As we reached it, Mia came down the stairs nearby and met us at the door.

"I need coffee," she complained.

"Me too," Nevaeh agreed, lifting her eyes to me hopefully. "Do you have time before your class?"

Grinning, I tossed an arm over Mia's shoulders and steered them in the direction of the campus café. "There is always time for coffee."

The café was crowded when we walked in. Mia grumbled unhappily as she pushed her way through students to get to the front so we could order. I kept closer to Nevaeh but made sure Mia was in my line of sight at all times. Old habits died hard, and I was constantly assessing a room for dangers to the girls as they studied the menu while a group of guys ordered in front of us.

They finally stepped out of the way so the girl at the cash register could take our orders, and I waited for the girls to make their selection before ordering a black coffee along with a bagel and handed over one of my credit cards.

"I can pay," Nevaeh said as she opened her backpack to grab her wallet.

"Your money's no good here, Kitten," I told her with a smirk as I took the receipt.

That only got me an adorable huff as she went to stand in line to get her drink.

"Grab my drink, guys. I'm going to find us a table," Mia instructed.

I swallowed my groan, my muscles tensing as I tried to watch her in the crowd now that she wasn't within arm's reach and still keep an eye on Nevaeh. I was so focused on Mia as she spoke to a group that appeared to be leaving their table that I didn't even realize someone had been talking to Nevaeh for several seconds.

"...should come. Our house is just off campus."

"I'll think about it," Nevaeh replied, and I snapped my head around so fast, I almost gave myself whiplash.

I took in the tool who was talking to her. Dark-wash jeans, a fraternity hoodie, and overly gelled hair. I put him at twenty, maybe a little older, with an addiction to teeth-whitening, given how blindingly white his teeth were when he flashed a smile at my kitten.

Nevaeh was barely paying attention to the guy, her gaze shifting toward the counter where the baristas were placing drinks and calling out names.

"Here, take my number and text me if you decide to come. I'll make sure you have a great time," the tool said, reaching out to take Nevaeh's phone from her hand.

I grabbed his wrist before he could touch it and twisted his arm behind his back. "She doesn't want your number, dumbass. The girl isn't interested."

"Braxton," she admonished, but there was more amusement in her voice than displeasure. "Don't break his arm."

"Dude," the tool whined. "I was just inviting her to a party. Geesh, relax."

"She doesn't want to go to your fucking party, asshole." I released him and pushed him back a few feet. "Get lost."

"Who the fuck are you anyway? Her brother?"

I took a menacing step toward him. "No, but I'll be your worst nightmare if you come near her again."

Soft hands touched my arm, stopping me from getting in the guy's face and, surprisingly, calming the rage that was just below the surface, ready to erupt and blow the café apart. "Excuse us," she murmured to the guy as she tugged me toward the counter. "Our drinks are ready."

I kept her hand in mine, asking the server for a tray so I could carry the drinks and my bagel without having to let her go. She took her drink and then glanced around for Mia.

"You don't have to scare every person who talks to me, you know," she commented as we made our way through the crowd toward the table where

Mia was camped out, waiting on us. She had her phone out, texting rapidly, and I figured she was either talking to her mom or Barrick. "Not everyone is the boogeyman who will snatch me and chop me into tiny pieces."

"You don't know that," I grumbled. "And I wasn't worried so much about the tiny pieces thing as him trying to get in your panties."

A tiny laugh escaped her, and she glanced up at me through her lashes. "If I didn't know better, I would say you were jealous." She laughed again and tugged her hand free of mine so she could pull out a chair for herself.

I stood there for a second, just looking down at her. Did she honestly think I *wasn't* jealous? The girl was smart as hell but apparently blind as a bat, even with her glasses on. I was so eaten up with jealousy whenever any guy looked at her, it was a wonder I didn't lose my shit every ten minutes.

Nevaeh Stevenson was mine; she just didn't realize it yet.

But it wasn't like I could stake a claim to her. Not when she was only sixteen fucking years old.

The next two years were going to be pure torture.

Chapter 3
Two Years Later

Braxton

I knew it was going to be a shit day when I heard the thunder booming and my alarm hadn't even gone off yet.

Sasha lifted her head, a whine leaving her, and I sat up so I could scratch her ears. My touch soothed her, and she began to relax again as she laid her head back down. Within minutes, she was back asleep at the end of my bed.

A soft tap on my door told me I wasn't going to get to attempt going back to sleep. "Yeah?" I called, and Mia stuck her head in, the light from the hall haloing around her.

"I'm making breakfast. Do you want some?"

I glanced at my alarm clock. I only had ten more minutes before I had to get up anyway. "Give me five minutes, and I'll be out."

"No rush," she said, flipping on my overhead light. "I just got a text that this storm has delayed our flight anyway."

And there it was—the real reason this was going to a shitty as fuck day.

Mia and her cousin were flying back to California. It was only for the weekend, so Nevaeh could celebrate her birthday with her family, but it reminded me that their time with me was limited.

Even more so for Nevaeh.

She had one more semester, and then she would graduate. Her parents expected her to come back to Cali for graduate school, and she hadn't argued.

Once May arrived, my sweet little kitten was going to leave me.

Scrubbing my hands over my face, I groaned.

"We'll be back Sunday night," Mia reminded me, compassion in her voice.

"But Barrick and I aren't going with you." Tossing back my covers, I moved to the edge of the bed and reached for my prosthesis. The cold, wet weather was making my leg hurt even more than usual.

"Am I going to get a lecture from you, too?" she asked with an exasperated huff. "Look, Barrick is taking us to the airport, where Nevaeh's grandfather's jet is already waiting on us. Marcus is on board and won't leave my side all weekend."

It was a relief that one of her old bodyguards would be with her during this trip, but that wasn't why I was having a hard time with them going without us this time.

Nevaeh was turning eighteen tomorrow, and I wasn't going to be with her to celebrate.

We'd had a huge dinner the night before in her honor, with cake and a taco buffet in the kitchen. Lyla and her little family had shown up, along with a few of Nevaeh's friends from school. Mia and I had spent the day making Nev's favorite cake and decorating it.

Neveah had had so much fun that she'd passed out on the couch after everyone left. I'd carried her to bed, and it took everything inside me to turn and walk back out of her room.

I was so close to the finish line, I could taste it. But there was still a little bit more to go.

It didn't matter that she was just days away from becoming legal. It wouldn't have mattered if she were minutes away. She was still seventeen. I couldn't touch her the way I'd been aching to.

Not yet.

And now, I had to fucking wait until she got back from visiting with her family before I could start showing her what she really meant to me.

"Are you guys going to eat or what?" Barrick called out from the kitchen. He sounded about as happy as I was, and I knew us not going with them was pissing him off just as much as it was me.

But both his and my parents were expecting us to show up later. Barrick's mom and stepfather had flown in just for this damn family get-together, and my parents had already given me the whole guilt trip because I'd blown off all the other major family events over the past few years. Thanksgiving, Christmas, Mother's and Father's Days. I'd sent presents when I was supposed to, called them once a month to let them know I was alive, but I tried to avoid face-to-face contact with them.

I was about to say fuck it all, pack a bag, and go with the girls.

To hell with my parents and whatever this was about. I wasn't in the right frame of mind to deal with their shit anyway. All they did was criticize and hover and make me feel like an incompetent ten-year-old who didn't know up from down. As if I needed them to hold my hand to cross the damn street.

Barrick was going because my mom knew how to lay on the guilt like crazy, but also because he had my back—and Mia had yelled at him and told him he had to go with me or else.

I didn't know what the "or else" entailed, but from the look on my cousin's face, I figured it was something more horrific than death, in his eyes.

"I better get out there," Mia muttered. "Mr. Grumpy is waiting on me to eat."

She turned to go, her long red hair flying over her shoulders. At the door, she paused. "I can stay if you really want me to, Brax. I have your back, you know that, right?"

"I know," I told her honestly. "And if anything, I'd rather you were out of the line of fire if things get ugly tonight. My parents aren't fans of Barrick, and you know why. Whatever they shoot at him could hit you, and I don't want to have to kill one of them if they hurt you in any way."

A sad smile tilted up her lips. "Call me after, okay? Let me know you're all right."

I nodded, and she closed the door on her way out. Alone again, I finally stood and cursed the pain. It quickly faded, but I was still clenching my teeth as I limped into my bathroom.

Ten minutes later, I walked into the kitchen to the smell of freshly brewed coffee and bacon. A plate was already set at my usual place at the table, loaded with eggs, sliced tomatoes, and toast. A mug full of steaming coffee the way I liked it was beside the plate, and I was already picking up my fork before I'd even sat down.

I was halfway through my breakfast when Nevaeh walked blurry-eyed into the kitchen. She didn't have her glasses on yet, and her left cheek still had the imprint of the lines from her pillowcase. Her long dark hair was pulled into a messy, tangled knot on top of her head, and she kept yawning in a way that was so damn adorable, I wanted to pet her.

"Where's the orange juice?" she mumbled sleepily, looking around the table through her lashes.

"Here it is, Kitten," I told her. Picking up the container, I poured some into the glass beside her plate that only had a single slice of toast on it.

As I set down the container, I noticed her jaw clenching and her eyes open fully. She shot me a glare before muttering her thanks and taking a sip.

Getting a hostile look from her set me on edge. What the hell had I done to earn a reaction like that just for pouring her damn juice?

Before I could ask what was wrong, Mia cut me off. "We have a little extra time, Nev. Momma texted me earlier to tell me Cole's pilot had to delay takeoff because of the weather. It's supposed to clear up this afternoon, so hopefully we can get in the air by then."

"Perfect. Maybe we should just cancel and do this next weekend. My parents will understand." She bit into her toast aggressively.

Yes, I wanted to shout.

But once again, Mia interrupted. "No, no. We should totally go this weekend. I mean, the jet is already here. It seems like a waste of resources not to use it like we are supposed to."

"I don't even care that it's my birthday. This is more for my mom than me," she complained. "I have so many finals to study for, Mia."

"Oh, please," Mia said with a roll of her big green eyes. "You already know more than your professors on every subject. You need to study like I need a hole in my head."

"Whatever." After another bite, Neveah tossed the toast back onto the plate and downed the rest of her juice. "I'm going to shower and finish up the rest of my packing."

As she stood, she gave me a scathing look I didn't understand.

"What did I miss?" I asked Barrick.

He shrugged as he shoveled food into his mouth.

No longer hungry, I pushed away my plate and stood. "I need to walk Sasha."

As I left the kitchen, I heard Mia tell Barrick, "It's going to be a really long weekend."

"Yeah," he agreed as the door shut behind me.

As I walked back to my bedroom, I saw Sasha going into Neveah's room. The German shepherd adored her. From their first meeting, Sasha had accepted Nev and considered her part of our family. She loved Mia too, but Neveah was her second-favorite person in the house.

Bypassing my room, I stopped outside Neveah's and watched them through the open door.

"Are you going to miss me, Sasha?" she asked the dog as she scratched the top of Sasha's head, earning a soft whine in answer. Nevaeh kissed her snout. "At least someone will," she muttered.

Straightening, she caught sight of me standing in the doorway. A sad look crossed her face, gutting me, before she masked it. She gave me a cool appraisal before walking to her closet.

"Are you mad at me?" I asked, walking into her room without asking permission. In the mood she was in, I doubted she would have given it anyway.

"What makes you think that?" she asked, not denying it.

"Just tell me what's wrong, Nevaeh," I told her, frustrated.

"There's nothing to tell," she said as she pulled a shirt off a hanger. Going to the case already open on the end of her bed, she folded the shirt and dropped it inside.

She made me want to pull my hair out. "Why are you being like this?" I demanded.

When she didn't answer, I caught hold of her wrist on her way back to the closet and gently tugged her around to face me. "Did I do something wrong?" She twisted her lips, and I made a pained sound in the back of my throat. "Kitten, I'm not above begging."

"Okay, fine."

I nearly groaned because I'd lived with Mia long enough to know those two words were a deadly combination. She said them whenever she was about to tear into Barrick and make his life a living hell until he could get her to forgive him. Hearing them coming from Nevaeh was enough to make me begin to sweat.

"I'm tired, Braxton. Tired of fighting with myself because our friendship has been slowly killing me for the past two years. It's fucking exhausting pretending like I don't like you. So, no, you haven't done anything wrong. This is all on me." Pulling her wrist free, she took two steps back. She blinked those beautiful, hypnotic blue-gray eyes at me, fighting tears. "I'm sorry," she whispered, looking down at her hands that she was clenching together. "I shouldn't have said anything."

Stunned by her confession, I stood there speechless. I wanted to grab her and kiss the breath out of her and make a few confessions of my own, but my conscience wouldn't let me. Not yet. She was still seventeen for sixteen more hours.

"Nevaeh," I rasped her name. "I—"

"No, don't say anything," she pleaded. "I don't think I could bear it. I just… I need to shower. Yeah, shower. You should go, Braxton. I think I've embarrassed myself enough for one day."

"Nev, just wait. Listen—"

"I really can't." Taking another step back, she shook her head, and twin tears spilled over her lashes. "Please, just go."

"Fuck this," I growled and grabbed her by the hips, jerking her into me roughly. "Do not run away from me, Kitten." Her mouth fell open, but at least her tears seemed to dry up. Those damn things made me crazy, and I couldn't think clearly whenever I saw them in her eyes. "Now, listen to me. You are seventeen, Nevaeh. Seven-fucking-teen. I know it's only for a few more hours, but I can't do what I've been thinking about and aching to do for too damn long. Not yet."

"Wh-what have you been aching to do?" she whispered, her breaths already coming in little pants that pushed her tits up against her old T-shirt.

I pressed my forehead to hers and inhaled deeply, pulling her fruity-floral scent into me. Her smell always calmed me, but I knew it was because my brain knew it as *her* scent. "Things I should have been shot for thinking about because you were too young. Now please, stop thinking stupid shit, and just give me a little more time before you go breaking your heart because you imagine I don't feel the same way you do."

Chapter 4
Nevaeh

The entire flight to California, I felt like my entire body was humming, and I couldn't seem to wipe the smile off my lips. All I could do was relive the moment in my bedroom that morning with Braxton.

For two years, I thought what I felt for him was unrequited. That I was the only one suffering in silence, wanting something I thought I could never have. Yet, Brax had hinted that he'd just been waiting until I was eighteen. He'd been aching for the same things I was.

I'd wanted to cancel my plans with my family and just stay home, see what would happen once the clock struck midnight and if Braxton would make a move after I turned the magical age of eighteen. But he seemed to know that and urged me to go, promising when I got back…

Well, he hadn't actually said what would happen when I got back. I knew he had his family obligation to deal with later that night, and he was stressed enough over that for me not to want to add more pressure onto his shoulders, so I hadn't demanded he tell me all the details I yearned for. Just knowing that *something* would happen was enough for the moment.

There was a black SUV waiting on the tarmac when the door of PopPop's jet was opened. Marcus exited first, making sure everything was clear before sticking his head back in and letting Mia know it was safe to leave our seats. Marcus wasn't expecting some sniper or a madman with a knife to attack us. It was more a horde of paparazzi that could jump out from behind some random vehicle he was concerned with.

Now that Mia and I were older, we were getting even more attention from photographers and other reporters, wanting all the dirty secrets on us since we were leading more separate lives from our parents. They didn't often get much, so they resorted to embellished half-truths. Their newest theory was that I had a secret addiction, saying the apple didn't fall far from the tree since my dad was a recovering alcoholic. They didn't seem to care that he'd been sober for twenty years.

As I descended the stairs of the jet, the back door of the SUV opened, and my mom jumped out. She screamed my name and started bouncing up and down, making me fear she would break the heel off one of her stiletto boots and hurt herself.

"Nev!" she squealed as I neared, and she threw her arms around me.

Her boots made her a few inches taller than me, and her eyes were a warm honey-brown, but other than that, we looked freakishly similar. Mom took great care of herself, and there wasn't a single line on her face that suggested she'd birthed five children who'd kept her and Daddy on their toes twenty-four seven for the past eighteen years. Her long dark hair was pulled up into a simple ponytail. She colored it to hide the few grays, the only real proof of her age.

"Happy almost birthday, my baby," she said as she pulled back enough to kiss my cheek. "Oh fuck, Nevaeh, how did you get to be eighteen so quickly?"

"Time flies when you're having fun," Mia commented from beside me, earning her a welcoming hug from Mom.

"How was your flight?" Mom asked as Marcus tossed our cases in the back of the SUV.

"Uneventful," I told her with a shrug.

47

"I doubt you would have noticed the back end of the plane exploding, you were so lost in your own wonderland," Mia said with a laugh. "It was so bumpy, I threw up for like an hour because of the weather over the Midwest."

Mom's eyes sparkled as we took our seats in the vehicle. "Hmm. I wonder why. It couldn't be because of a certain retired Marine, now could it?"

I felt my cheeks heat, but I wasn't about to lie to her. "Maybe."

"So…" Mom crossed her legs and turned slightly to face me. "What's the verdict on that avenue currently? The boy smarten up yet?"

"Mom," I huffed. "Really, it's none of your business."

"Bullshit. I just want to know if you two are going to become a thing. And if so, are you still going to go to grad school here or back in Virginia?"

I sighed as I pulled on my seat belt, and Mia took her place beside me. When I glanced at her, I noticed she looked a little green, making me wonder just how upset her stomach really was from the flight. Sweat beaded on her upper lip, and she wiped her hand across it, giving me a grimace before snapping her own belt in place. I knew she didn't always travel well when it came to flying, but I thought I'd heard her in her bathroom earlier that morning being sick…

My eyes widened when she winked at me, but I kept my mouth shut. Maybe she had a reason other than my birthday celebration with the family to want to come home to see her parents.

"Nev." Mom pulled my focus back to her. "Are you going to come home or not?"

"As of right now, I'm coming home for grad school," I informed her, storing away the possibility of Mia being pregnant for when we were alone.

My answer didn't seem to assuage Mom's curiosity. Instead, we were subjected to question after question about what was happening back in Virginia on the way to Mia's house. The driver dropped her and Marcus off without us going inside, and then we made our way home.

Dad was in Downtown LA with the rest of the Demons working on some new music for a movie soundtrack they'd been asked to contribute to. Normally all my siblings went wherever either of my parents went. A nanny was never something I'd experienced growing up because Mom and Dad wanted to be fully hands-on with all of us. So it was unusual for Mom to show up at the airport alone, but she'd been asking Mia and me so many questions, I hadn't had the chance to ask her where my brother and sisters were.

I finally got the opportunity a few miles from home. "Where is everyone?"

"They all had friends to visit. They'll be home later tonight, though." She said it so casually, but I was sure I'd seen something in her eyes. I couldn't read it, and for some reason, that set off alarm bells inside me.

"I'm making all your favorites for dinner tonight," she informed me, hurriedly changing the subject as the driver pulled into the driveway.

Mom normally drove a minivan and Dad had his SUV, but when she had to go to the airport or anywhere in LA by herself, she called for a driver—something she didn't like to do often.

She liked a simple life, one in which she took care of every aspect of her own life. It didn't matter that she and Dad had millions in the bank, or that she was PopPop's only heir and would one day inherit all his money and everything else tied to Cole Steel's name, including his share of the Steel Entrapment brand that still brought in a decent profit every year.

As expected, my room was exactly as I'd left it during my last visit, which had been for a few short weeks over the summer. The bed was perfectly made, with all my favorite stuffed animals against the pillows. My favorite Demon's Wings poster, which had my mom and all the other Demon wives on it instead of Dad and my uncles, was hanging up on the wall over my desk, reminding me what a badass woman looked and acted like.

My desk had a stack of books on the edge along with my desktop computer. There wasn't a single speck of dust in the entire room, telling me that Mom had come in at least once a week to clean. It also told me that Arella and my other siblings had thankfully stayed out.

Which was a good thing, so I didn't have to kill any of them, especially Arella.

After washing up and changing my clothes, I walked downstairs to the smell of Mom already cooking. The scent of garlic bread and rich tomato sauce filled the air, and I followed my nose to the kitchen, where she was standing over the stove, making a huge pot of spaghetti.

As I entered the room, Mom didn't immediately notice my presence, and I saw just how tense her shoulders were. Her head was bent, as if the weight of the world were pressing down on her and she couldn't find the strength to hold it up any longer.

I'd never seen my mom like that before. She was a strong woman, my first and true mentor, and I couldn't comprehend what could be so wrong that she couldn't hold her head up.

"Mom?" I asked and watched her jump.

Turning to face me, she laughed and pressed a hand to her chest. "You scared the hell out of me, Nev. Damn, I guess I've gotten so used to you not being home that I forgot for a second. Sorry, sweetheart. Do you need something?"

"For you tell me what's wrong," I told her, not buying for a second that she'd forgotten I was in the house.

Her smile died, and she turned back to dinner. "Nothing's wrong, silly."

"Mom."

"Okay, maybe I'm feeling my age because tomorrow I will actually have an eighteen-year-old child." She laughed again, but I could easily hear the strain in it.

"Seriously, Mom. Since when do you worry about your age?" I knew she was lying, but for the moment, I would let her pretend. If she didn't want to tell me, then maybe Daddy would let me know what was wrong with her.

"It's a new development." Mom played it off with a wave of her hand. "I've realized that with one child out in the world finding herself, the others will soon follow. And then all too soon, it will just be me and your father in this huge house with no babies to care for."

There was real sadness in her voice now, and it made my heart clench for her. "Relax, Mom. I'm sure by the time Damien is out of the house, at least one of us will have given you grandkids to spoil."

She shot me a wicked grin over her shoulder. "Maybe sooner than expected if you and Braxton figure yourselves out."

"Mom…" I whined even as the thought produced the most unusual feeling of rightness I'd ever experienced. "Please do not say shit like that in front of Daddy."

Laughing, she bent and pulled a pan of crusty garlic bread out of the oven. "Go set the table. It's us and Dad for dinner, and he just called to say he was on his way. Should be here in less than twenty minutes."

Doing as I was told, I grabbed the plates and silverware and set the kitchen table since it was just the three of us. There was a huge table that could potentially seat fifty in the gigantic dining room that we only ever used when we had family dinners with our extended family. But that didn't happen often, so the dining room table was more often than not an arts and crafts table that Mom and Arella constantly had covered.

By the time Mom had placed a bowl of salad on the table, I heard the front door open.

Surprised that he hadn't come in through the garage, I took off running and threw myself into Daddy's arms the second I saw him. He let out a pained groan as I squeezed him, and I laughed, thinking he was playing around.

Until I looked up at his face and saw his skin was gray, and even though he was grinning down at me, he couldn't hide the pain in his eyes.

"I'm sorry," I hurriedly apologized. "I didn't mean to be so rough."

"It's okay, sweetheart," he assured me, kissing the top of my head and giving me a squeeze in return. "I've missed you so damn much."

"Dray, dinner is ready," Mom called out.

"Coming, Angel." Tossing one arm around my shoulders, he guided me back into the kitchen. "Let me wash my hands, and we can eat."

I took my place and picked up my napkin while Mom dished out the spaghetti onto each of our plates. As Daddy joined us at the table, he kissed her temple, telling her he loved and missed her. She leaned into the touch of his lips, and before she closed her eyes, I thought I saw a sheen of tears in her honey-brown eyes.

But when she opened them again, it was gone, making me wonder if I'd imagined it.

"How did work go today?" she asked as she took her place at the table and reached for the salad dressing.

"We finally decided on what sound we wanted to go with for that song Nik and I have been working on all week," Daddy told her before stuffing his mouth full with spaghetti. "It sounds wicked."

I listened to them talk as I ate, watching them both. But the longer dinner went on, the more tension I could feel radiating from both of my parents. It set my nerves on edge, and I began to watch them even more closely.

That's when I started noticing the changes in Daddy. There were bruises on his right forearm, which surprised me because I couldn't ever remember him having a bruise on him. It took longer to notice the weight loss because it was subtle, but eventually, I did.

And that was when I noticed the slight discoloration of his eyes. They had a yellow tinge to them.

"Are you sick?" I blurted out, unable to stop the words.

Mom's fork made a loud *clank* as it hit her plate, her fingers having lost their hold on it as soon as I opened my mouth. Daddy's eyes met mine, and I read the answer there even as he reached over and covered Mom's shaking hand, giving it a gentle squeeze.

"We wanted to tell you ourselves," he said with a grim twist of his mouth. "Yes, Nevaeh. I'm sick."

"But…" I swallowed hard, feeling tears burning my eyes. My mind ran through the list of visible symptoms I could see. Bruising. Weight loss.

Jaundice. I'd hurt him when I hugged him earlier, and I tried to remember exactly where my arms had been when I'd squeezed. But I wasn't a damn doctor, and nothing was coming to mind because I wasn't studying to go into the medical field. "What's wrong with you?"

He glanced at Mom and sighed heavily before turning his gaze back to me. "Remember when I had that fender bender back in August? It was right after you went back to Virginia for the fall semester."

"You said you didn't get hurt," I recalled aloud.

He'd been a passenger in Uncle Jesse's SUV along with my other uncles when they'd gotten rear-ended on their way home from the studio. No one had gotten hurt from what Mom told me right after it happened.

"The seat belt caused some bruising across my abdomen, and I started having some pain. A lot of pain, if I'm being honest. Your mom made me go in for tests." He swallowed hard and let out a strained laugh. "My past caught up with me, sweetheart. All those years of drinking caused some pretty significant damage. I have Stage 4 liver disease. I've had it for decades and didn't even realize it. If it weren't for the accident, I still might not have found out."

"What?" I didn't understand, or maybe I just didn't want to understand. My mind couldn't wrap itself around the fact that he was sick, let alone what disease he had. But it was starting to make sense, even though I really didn't want it to. Because if there was a name for his illness, a diagnosis, then that made it real.

And I didn't want it to be fucking real.

"It's okay, sweetheart," Mom finally spoke, but her voice was thick with tears. "Because Daddy is getting a new liver, and he will be just fine."

I blinked at her in surprise. "Do you know how long people are on those damn transplant lists?" That much, I did know. "It could take years before he gets one and—"

"Uncle Shane is giving me part of his, Nev," Daddy interrupted before I could start spouting off statistics.

"Really?" I whispered and finally lost the battle against my tears, letting them flow freely. "Are you sure he's a good enough match? If he's not, I'll give you part of mine, Daddy. I know we have the same blood type. Surely we would be a better genetic match."

"We've already had all the tests done, honey. He's a positive match."

"But maybe it would be better if I did it anyway. Let me do some research and figure out if it's better if a child donates an organ for you to have a higher chance of not rejecting it than a sibling donating." I picked up my phone, already typing rapidly.

Daddy reached across the table and snatched my phone from my hand. Placing it facedown on the table, he glared at me. "You are not donating anything. Neither are your sisters or your brother. This is happening because of my mistakes, and I'm not going to put any of you through that kind of pain and danger to fix them. The only reason I agreed to accept Shane's offer was because your mom begged me to."

"Are you crazy?" I didn't mean to yell, but I was so upset, I couldn't seem to control the volume of my voice. "Daddy, if the chance of survival is higher for me to give you a part of my liver, then of course, you need to take it. Don't be stubborn. A small amount of pain is nothing if it means you get better."

"I said no, Nevaeh. And that's final." He picked up his glass of water and downed half of it before pushing his chair back and standing. "Sorry, Angel. I'm not hungry."

I watched him go before scrubbing my hands across my cheeks and finally looking over at Mom. "P-please. Let me do this. Just let me do the research, talk to the doctors, figure something out…"

But she shook her head. "He's already made up his mind. It took weeks of me crying and pleading and making all kinds of ugly threats before he agreed to take Shane up on his offer." Reaching over, she covered my ice-cold hand with her own. "I know this is scary. I'm terrified right now myself. But all we can do is accept your father's decisions and pray everything works out."

I couldn't accept it, though. "But if I'm a better genetic match—"

"Honey, Uncle Shane's tests showed that they are a perfect match. The doctors said they couldn't possibly have gotten a better genetic match if they'd searched for a hundred years. Because, trust me,

Aunt Natalie and Aunt Jenna both got tested, and while they were matches, they didn't come anywhere close to what Shane's is." She stood and walked around the table to hug me. "It's going to be okay, Nevaeh. We won't lose him."

I pressed my face into her chest and finally released the sob that felt like it had been clogging my throat from the moment I realized something was wrong with my daddy. "How can you know?" I choked out, clinging to her.

"I don't," she whispered, her voice trembling. "But I can't think of any other outcome. If I do, I will definitely lose my mind."

Chapter 5
Nevaeh

Mom made me finish dinner, but I could barely choke it down. Once the plate was almost empty, I excused myself and, grabbing my phone, ran up to my room.

All I could think about was talking to Braxton. I needed him, but just getting to hear his voice would be enough for the moment. I hit connect on his name in my call history and waited.

He was three hours ahead of me, and I knew he was at his parents' for that damn family thing with Barrick, but I hoped he would still answer. He didn't, and I felt a fresh wave of tears flood from my eyes as I fought back a sob.

Swallowing it before either of my parents heard, I called my next best choice of people I needed to talk to.

Mia picked up on the second ring, sounding like she was in the process of being sick again. "Wasn't expecting to hear from you," she muttered, and I heard the toilet flush seconds before a faucet was turned on. "Figured your parents would have you telling them minute-by-minute details of what's been going on since you last saw them."

"I guess your mom hasn't told you, then," I said, sniffling.

"Tell me what?" she said loudly, then groaned. "Hold on a second. I have to puke again… Oh gods."

I grimaced at the sound of her retching and then dry heaving, but I stayed on the phone because I desperately needed to talk to her.

It was several minutes later before she came back on the line. "Okay, I think I'm good for the moment. Fuck, they should call this crap all-day sickness."

"So, you really are pregnant?" I whispered just to make sure no one heard by accident.

"Apparently," she said with a sigh. "I took a test two days ago. Remember when I had strep about two months ago? Well, those damn antibiotics canceled out my birth control."

"Have you told your parents yet?"

"Daddy just got home, and Momma is on her way. I want to tell them together. Jagger is already making jokes, though, and I'm about to murder the little asshole if he doesn't shut the hell up." Another sigh. "I'm also telling them Barrick and I are moving up the wedding."

"What?" I sat up a little straighter. "But you guys took forever setting the date. I thought he wanted you to graduate before you got married."

"Yeah, well, he shouldn't have knocked me up. I know my parents weren't married when they had me. I was the damn flower girl, for fuck's sake. But I want to share Barrick's last name before this little one makes an appearance. Which I think is in July if my math is right. Hell, I'm not a hundred percent sure."

"When do you plan on getting married, then?" I asked skeptically. "Because you know Aunt Emmie has already been planning a huge wedding for you guys."

"Well, that's the thing. I never wanted a big wedding. I was thinking of having something simple here at the house before the spring term starts. That will give me time to find a dress and let everyone know where and when, have the wedding, and go on a short honeymoon before classes begin." She sounded so excited for it, I didn't have the heart to tell her that her mother was going to freak when Mia laid out her plans for the wedding she wanted.

"Good luck with that," was all I said.

"Now, what should I have been told? You sounded upset when you first called."

I closed my eyes. For just a moment, I'd been able to turn off the devastation that was making my entire being quake with fear and dread and heartbreak. But now, I couldn't avoid any of those emotions as a fresh wave of tears stung my eyes. "Mia, Daddy is sick."

"What do you mean, sick?" she demanded. "Like, he has a cold?"

"No," I whispered.

"Okay, you need to explain to me what kind of sick Uncle Drake is right now because I'm starting to freak out."

Sucking in a deep breath that did nothing to calm my emotions, I dove into the deep end and told her everything I currently knew. By the time I was done, I could hear her crying softly.

"Oh my gods. Nevaeh, I'm so sorry. This is… I can't wrap my head around it, so I can only imagine what you are feeling right now." She sniffled and cleared her throat. "Is there anything I can do? I mean… I don't really know what I mean. No one has ever really been ill in our family, not like this, and I don't understand what needs to be done at a time like this."

"Mostly, I just want to talk to Braxton," I told her. "But he didn't answer when I called him."

"Yeah, Barrick didn't answer either when I called him right before I started puking my guts out once again." She muttered a curse under her breath. "I bet Braxton's parents are making them both feel like they're about six years old right now. They're good about pulling the guilt trip. They still blame Barrick for Braxton losing his leg."

"Do you think he will be okay?" I asked, worried about him.

"Honey, you just found out your dad needs a new liver, and you're worried about Braxton dealing with his loser parents?" She laughed ever so softly. "Sounds like you've got it bad, babe."

"I do," I confessed. "I love him. I think…I think I always have. How stupid is that?"

"You're asking me?" Mia snorted. "It was kind of love at first sight for me with Barrick, so I would never say that what you feel for him is anywhere close to stupid. Intense, sure. But never stupid."

From downstairs, I heard at least one of my siblings yelling and realized they'd made it home from their friends' houses. I had a feeling at least one of them knew what was going on with Daddy, and I was going to tear her hair out of her pretty little head for keeping me in the dark.

"I have to go kill Arella," I told Mia. "If you hear from Barrick or Braxton, could you pass on the message that I need to talk to Braxton?"

"Will do. I'm going to go paint the toilet a lovely shade of puke once more before Momma gets home. Wish me luck that no one puts a hit out on my fiancé when they hear my news."

"Yeah, good luck with that," I told her with a dry laugh, only to hear her retching again.

Hanging up to let her be miserable in peace, I tossed my phone onto the bed and jumped up. I sprinted across the room and out the door just in time to meet Arella about to enter her own bedroom across the hall.

My sixteen-year-old sister looked even more like our mother than I did, with the same natural highlights in her dark hair and the sprinkle of freckles across her nose. She'd inherited Daddy's artistic genes, but it was acting that was her real passion. Something Mom hated, but she had never stood in Arella's way when she'd started taking classes to improve what was a surprisingly natural talent.

Not even giving Arella time to realize I was behind her, I grabbed her by the back of her hair and twisted my fingers in the thick locks. She screamed in pain and tried to turn around to grab my own hair, but I pushed her into her room and slammed the door shut before flipping the lock.

I dragged my sister across the room and pushed her down onto her bed before finally releasing her. Seeing strands of her hair in my fist didn't give me the satisfaction it would have during one of our usual hair-pulling fights, though.

Arella turned over onto her back and glared up at me. "What was that for, bitch?"

I bent so I was in her face, and her hot breath steamed up my glasses. Pushing them onto my forehead, I fisted my hands at my sides to keep from pulling her hair again. "Why didn't you warn me that Daddy is sick?" I snarled.

Her eyes widened then filled with tears. "Be-because they made me promise not to tell you anything. They wanted to explain everything themselves without you doing that crazy brain thing of yours and trying to figure it all out on your own."

"You still should have told me." My voice wobbled, and I dropped down onto the edge of her bed. "I thought we promised no secrets."

She sighed heavily and sat up. She wrapped her arms around me and rested her head on my shoulder. "It wasn't my secret to share," she explained softly. "Mom and Daddy have been stressed enough, and I didn't want to add more to their plate by going against their wishes and telling you behind their backs."

"Yeah," I muttered, wiping at a stray tear that dripped down my face. "I get it." I pulled the strands free that were tangled around my fingers and let them float to her floor. "Sorry about your hair."

She grunted. "You should be. The only reason I'm letting this pass is because you're upset about Daddy and tomorrow is your birthday. Consider my not retaliating my present to you. There. You're welcome."

I shoved her onto her back and stood. "Whatever. I'm not scared of your skinny ass." I flipped her off on my way out of her room.

"What was Arella screaming about just now?" Mom asked as she came up the stairs.

"Nothing," I told her. "She was just being dramatic like always."

Back in my room, I picked up my phone in the hope Braxton might have called, but it was free of any messages. Putting my glasses back in place, I tried calling him again, and then again when I went to voice mail.

Realizing I wasn't likely to speak to him at all that night, I finally sent him a text.

Nevaeh: Today has royally sucked. I really need to hear your voice right now. Please…just call me. I don't care how late it is. I… Just… Please?

Chapter 6
Braxton

I hadn't worn a suit in so long, I felt like I was being choked by a toddler with the tie of my tux as soon as I put the damn thing on.

Normal families didn't require a person to show up wearing black-tie attire for a damn family get-together. My family was anything but normal, however. They flashed their money around like it was an accessory, demanding the world take notice. I'd hated the pretentiousness of it growing up.

After witnessing Mia's and Nevaeh's families at their annual Christmas party for the last few years, seeing people who were just as rich as my own parents act like money wasn't the most important thing in the world, I'd looked back on my childhood and hated it even more.

Barrick grabbed a glass of champagne off a tray one of the many caterers was carrying around the lower level of my parents' mansion and tossed back its entire contents in one gulp before replacing the expensive stemware and grabbing another.

"How long until they make their damn announcement and we can go?" I muttered, wishing I could start throwing back a few drinks myself. But I'd been in pain all day, and I never risked mixing my medication with alcohol.

"Knowing your folks, probably won't be for hours. Fuck, I'm starving. These canapes are disgusting. Let's grab some burgers on the way home." Pulling out his phone, he checked for texts from Mia and muttered a curse when he read something on his screen. "Dude, do you have any missed calls? Mia says Nevaeh is trying to reach you."

I pulled out my phone, saw a few missed calls and a text lighting up the screen. My eyes scanned over the message and my gut clenched.

Kitten: *Today has royally sucked. I really need to hear your voice right now. Please…just call me. I don't care how late it is. I… Just… Please?*

Glancing around, I saw the library appeared empty. As I entered, I shut the door and leaned back against it since there wasn't a lock on it. Swiping my thumb over her name, I closed my eyes and waited for her to answer.

"Hello?" Her voice sounded husky with tears and sleep, putting me on red alert.

"What's wrong, Kitten?" I asked softly, when I wanted to demand answers. Who upset her and made my sweet little Nevaeh cry?

"Brax," she whispered and sniffled. "Sorry, I guess I must have fallen asleep."

"Why are you crying?" I clenched my hand around my phone, but I quickly relaxed it a little when I heard something begin to crack.

"I got the worst news tonight." Her voice broke, and then I heard her sucking in a shuddery breath. That sound made it impossible for me to breathe until she spoke again. "Oh God, Braxton. I…I really wish you were here right now."

"Baby."

There was a knock on the door. "Brax, man. Your parents are about to make an announcement."

I pulled the phone away from my mouth. "Fuck them," I called through the door. "This is more important."

"Shit," Nevaeh muttered. "I'm interrupting your thing with your parents. You should go. Can you call me back later?"

"No. I don't care about them and their big announcement." Nothing they had to say mattered more than finding out what was wrong with my girl. "Talk to me, Nev. What news did you get?"

"It's my dad," she said, and a sob escaped her. I listened as she told me how sick her dad was and that he needed a new liver. I could hear the fear and heartbreak in her voice, and I felt like I was suffocating because there was nothing I could do to take her pain away.

There was another knock on the door I was leaning against. "Dude, you seriously need to get out here and stop this before your parents fuck up your life."

"Y-you should go," Nevaeh said, having heard my cousin. "I need to go talk to my brother and sisters anyway."

"I wish there was something I could do, Kitten."

"Just hearing your voice was enough," she whispered. "Now, get back to your party. I'll call you tomorrow."

"Baby—"

"Go," she commanded softly.

"Brax!" Barrick growled from the other side of the door. "Seriously. Get out here now."

Muttering a curse, I told Nevaeh I'd talk to her tomorrow and jerked the door open. Barrick's jaw was set, and he grabbed me by the shoulders and pulled me out of the library. After he turned me to face the stairs, it took me a second to understand what I was looking at.

My mother, clad in a dress that probably cost the equivalent of a compact car, dripping in diamonds, and with her hair and makeup her idea of perfection, stood beside my father with a glass of champagne in hand. His tux was tailored to his lanky frame, his wire-rimmed glasses perched on his nose as he lifted his own glass of expensive French champagne toward the woman standing to his left.

I narrowed my eyes on the woman. Dressed in a simple floor-length black dress, she had her blond hair pulled into a delicate twist at the right side of her head. It took me a second to realize who she was because I hadn't seen her in… Fuck, I couldn't even remember how long it had been.

"Is that—?"

"Yup," Barrick growled.

"What the hell is she doing here?" I bit out.

"Officially announcing your engagement."

"Fuck."

"There he is," my father said with a chuckle, his eyes falling on me. He waved me forward, as if he expected me to fall in line with their newest scheme to try to run my life.

My eyes landed back on Darcy Hamilton, and I cursed my own past idiocies. Darcy was my high school girlfriend. And like most guys that age, I'd thought more with my dick than my brain. I thought because the sex was good and she pretended to love me, we would be together forever. I proposed on her eighteenth birthday, and even though we were young, both her parents and mine had actually endorsed our marriage.

Then I'd enlisted in the Marines. Darcy changed, and I realized she was trying to manipulate me just as much as my parents were. But it wasn't until I lost my leg that I saw how shallow she really was. She dumped me, saying she wasn't the type of woman who could spend her life caring for an invalid husband because she didn't think I would walk again.

To be honest, she hadn't broken my heart when she gave me back the ring. If anything, I'd been relieved I was able to get rid of her so easily. I'd spent the months of my deployment trying to figure out how to break off our engagement without stirring up more shit with my parents.

I walked through the crowd, all eyes on me. People I hadn't seen in years and whose names I couldn't remember for the life of me grinned, and a few patted me on the back, offering me congratulations. Climbing the stairs, I turned my full focus on my father.

"What the hell is going on?" I demanded in a voice low enough that only the three other people on the stairs could hear me.

Darcy linked her arm through mine and laid her head on my shoulder, her blue eyes gazing up at me adoringly. I knew it was an act she was putting on for the crowd, and it irritated the hell out of me. All I could think was that my beautiful little kitten was thousands of miles away, hurting because she was scared she was going to lose her father, and these people had kept me from being with her because they wanted to announce my marriage to this spoiled little bitch?

Fuck that.

"Darling, we know you've been dragging your feet about setting a date for the wedding," my mother said with a beaming smile for the crowd below. "So, we thought we would just take all the stress away and do it for you."

"Darcy and I aren't even together," I gritted out. "I forgot all about her until just now."

Darcy made a pained noise and pouted up at me. "Brax, don't be mean."

I shrugged her off and took two steps away from her. "I'm not in the mood to play any of your games. Tell these people the truth, and leave me the hell alone."

My father clenched his jaw. "You will marry Darcy. It's part of the merger her father and I agreed to. Your marriage will only solidify our new joint corporation."

"Fuck your new corporation," I told him. "I won't be a pawn you can use to make more money with Hamilton. Tell everyone you were joking. Now."

"Darling—" my mother started to scold me, but I turned to face the crowd to do it myself.

"Everyone, I'm sorry, but my parents have it wrong. Darcy and I are not getting married—"

"Until after Christmas," Darcy interrupted, and for the first time in my life, I actually wanted to cause a woman bodily harm. "Because we want to move in to our new house and get the nursery decorated before the big wedding."

Collective gasps and cheers went up at her basically announcing her pregnancy. What the actual fuck?

But as I opened my mouth to tell everyone it was all a misunderstanding, I saw cameras flashing in our direction and knew the story of Braxton Collins and Darcy Hamilton's upcoming wedding and parenthood was going to be on all the trashy gossip sites by morning.

Barrick was right.

My parents were going to ruin my life.

Chapter 7
Nevaeh

My head was foggy when I woke up the next morning.

After talking to Braxton the night before, I felt like I could breathe a little easier again and was able to talk to my sisters and brother rationally. As rationally as I could while being pissed at each and every one of them for keeping Daddy's illness from me.

Arella hadn't wanted to put more stress on our parents, I got that, but they still should have told me. Having the entire country between us shouldn't mean that our loyalty to each other disappeared. We were close, and yeah, we fought like crazy at times—especially Arella and me—but we'd always promised we would have each other's backs.

Once I stopped bitching at them and they apologized contritely and promised it wouldn't happen again, I'd gone back to my room and done some research. I found out that it wouldn't matter if it were a child or a sibling that matched as long as the genetic match was a good one. According to Mom, Daddy and Uncle Shane were as good as it got from what the doctors told them. That was a relief at least.

Once I learned all I could on what to expect, and what Daddy should and shouldn't be doing to prepare for surgery, I finally passed out in bed. That had been close to three in the morning.

Blurry-eyed, I glanced at my clock and saw it was almost noon. Groaning, I got out of bed and walked half blind into the bathroom to shower.

By the time I got downstairs in search of something to eat, the rest of the house had been up for hours, and it seemed we had guests.

Aunt Lucy and Aunt Layla were sitting in the kitchen with Mom, both of them drinking tea. Both of them were Mom's biological sisters, but Aunt Layla and Uncle Jesse had adopted Aunt Lucy when she was a little girl and raised her as their own. We had a weird family, but I loved it that way. Normal just seemed boring to me, and boring was unacceptable.

"Happy birthday!" Aunt Lucy greeted as she stood and practically bounced over to wrap her arms around me. Both she and Aunt Layla were shorter than Mom and even more so than me. With her smaller size, Lucy didn't look like she was a mother of two. She always laughed when people told her she looked like a teenager, and she said it was because her doting husband's love kept her looking young.

I hugged her back, then accepted one from Aunt Layla.

"We're going shopping," Mom informed me with a smile. "I think you need a new outfit for your party tonight, don't you?"

"I'm not really up to shopping, Mom," I told her. What I really wanted to do was crawl into my dad's lap and soak up his love for a few hours while we watched crappy old movies.

"Your dad went golfing with your uncles," Mom informed me as if she could read my mind. "The younger kids are all over at Shane and Harper's, and Arella is getting ready to go with us. So, hurry your ass up. We're leaving in five minutes."

Sighing, I looked down at my outfit. Skinny jeans with a hole in the left knee and the hoodie I'd stolen from Braxton the first week I'd moved in with him. It was my favorite hoodie, and sometimes I slept in it when it got really cold back in Northern Virginia.

"I'm ready," I told Mom.

"Really?" Her brown eyes skimmed over my attire, and her lips pressed into a firm line. "Don't you want to change that hoodie?"

"This is Braxton's hoodie. I'm not changing it."

Her eyes softened, and a sly grin teased at her lips. "Of course it is. Okay, then. Get your beautiful butt in the van while I go make your sister hurry up."

"We're meeting Emmie and Mia at the mall," Aunt Layla informed me as we entered the garage and got into Mom's minivan. It was spacious and always clean, no matter how hard Damien tried to destroy the interior every day.

I climbed into the back with Aunt Lucy, and by the time I had my seat belt on, Mom appeared with Arella. My younger sister was dressed in a skirt I knew our dad would have freaked over and a red sweater with thigh-high black boots. Her hair was pulled into a ponytail, but she'd curled the ends. With the makeup she had on, she looked like she was ready for a date, not a simple day of shopping with her family.

Knowing Arella, though, I imagined she was probably expecting to see friends from school at the mall, and she didn't like to look anything but perfect around them.

We met Mia and Aunt Emmie in the mall's garage. Marcus and Rodger, their bodyguards, were with them but thankfully dressed in casual clothes rather than their normal suits.

As soon as she saw me, Aunt Emmie threw her arms around me. "Happy birthday, sweetheart," she said as she kissed my cheek.

"Thanks, Aunt Em," I murmured.

As she stepped back, she put her arm around Mia's waist. "Where to first?"

"Coffee," Mom spoke. "I need caffeine stat."

Mia's face turned green, and she muttered a small oath but put on a bright smile and nodded her head along with the others who agreed that we needed to arm ourselves with drinks before we started shopping.

As we walked into the mall, I dropped back to talk to Mia. "How are you feeling?" I asked quietly.

She only gave me a look that was full of misery. "Kill me now."

"Is it that bad?"

As soon as we walked through the mall entrance, she groaned and put her hand to her nose. "Worse," she muttered. "These food smells are killing me."

"But the food court is on the third floor," I reminded her.

"Yeah, but it seems like my sense of smell is amplified. Mom told me she had the worst morning sickness when she was pregnant."

I glanced at the others as they walked ahead of us. "You told her?"

"Just her," Mia said with a nod. "Not Daddy yet."

I stopped and turned to face her. "Mia, don't you think it's time to finally forgive your dad? It's been two years, and he's tried time and again to earn back your trust."

Her chin trembled for a moment before she shook her head. "I've tried. Believe me, I really have. It's just hard to get over what he did, Nev."

"I understand, but you forgave Barrick. Why can't you do the same for Uncle Nik?"

"Because…" She clenched her jaw and swallowed hard. "Because he broke my heart more than Barrick ever could."

That made a lot of sense to me. Having your heart broken by your father—the man who was your first hero, the first man to ever love you wholeheartedly—that was a million times worse than any other heartbreak. Mia lost a part of herself when Uncle Nik betrayed her, and I didn't know if she was ever going to get it back.

"Anyway," Mia said as she put her arm through mine and we started walking again. "I thought maybe Barrick and I could do a cute little baby announcement for Daddy. Maybe a Christmas present or something that announces his impending grandfatherhood."

"Yeah, that would be nice," I agreed.

For the next two hours, we shopped and had lunch in the food court. Mia tried to eat a slice of pizza, but two bites in, she had to excuse herself. Thankfully, the bathrooms were close by because she had to make a run for it.

All the moms at the table shared a look with Aunt Emmie, who grinned and nodded her head. But no one said anything about it. Not even when Mia returned from the bathroom fifteen minutes later, looking less green but sweaty. They all pretended nothing out of the ordinary had happened.

"Well, we should get going," Aunt Emmie announced as she got to her feet. "I have a few things to pick up before the party tonight." She kissed the top of Arella's head then gave me a hug. "Enjoy the rest of your afternoon, babes."

Mia gave me a wave, wiping at the perspiration on her upper lip as she walked with her mom and the two bodyguards toward the escalators.

"Mom," Arella said as she pushed away her plate of half-eaten Japanese. "Palmer is downstairs. Can I go with her? She'll drop me off, and I promise I'll be home in time for the party."

Without hesitating, Mom nodded. "But if you're late, you're grounded. I mean it, Arella."

She made an X on her chest. "I promise." Jumping up, she kissed Mom's cheek and skipped off toward the escalators as well.

"That girl is going to get in trouble, Lana," Aunt Layla said with a laugh.

Mom snorted. "When isn't she getting in trouble? Drake put an extra tracker on her phone, though. Seeing as she disabled the first one so she could go to some party a few weeks ago."

I wasn't surprised by my sister's antics. She was born to cause trouble. Of the five of us, Arella was the wildest, and I knew the majority of Daddy's gray hair was because of her.

Half listening to the others talking, I pulled out my phone to see if I had a text from Braxton. There was nothing, and I tried to push down my disappointment. I'd already texted him twice, even snapped a picture of myself in the changing room trying on the new dress I'd picked out for the party in the hope of getting a flirty response. I should have known I wouldn't; Braxton had never flirted before, but a girl could dream, damn it.

"Four of the most beautiful women I have ever seen are sitting here with no man in sight," a deep voice I knew well announced, making everyone at the table but me laugh as Jordan Moreitti appeared at the end of the table. "I knew this was my lucky day, but damn, ladies."

I rolled my eyes so hard, his dark eyes landed on me, and I stuck my tongue out at him before flipping him off. He was Mia's best friend, so we saw him a lot back in Virginia. Probably more often than his parents did since he spent his time either in Italy working in his father's company or visiting Mia.

"What are you doing in this part of the country?" I asked. "Last time I saw you, you were trying your hardest to avoid this place."

"Needed to see Mia, and lo and behold, she was in this godforsaken dump."

"Yeah, California is a cesspool." Rolling my eyes again, I tossed my napkin at him. "You just missed her."

He shrugged. "I'll catch her later. It's your birthday, right?" I nodded. "Maybe your mom would be okay if I took you shopping for a present."

"Mom would be fine with that," she said with a wink as she and my aunts stood and gathered their bags. "Party starts at seven. Don't be late." She patted Jordan on the arm. "And you are more than welcome to join us, sweetie."

"I would love to, Mrs. Stevenson," he told her before accepting a hug from Aunt Layla.

"Perfect. See you two tonight, then."

I watched them go until they were on the escalator, then turned back to Jordan. "What are you really doing in California?"

His mouth thinned, and he mumbled, "Hiding out."

That made me crack up. "Figures. You're such a manwhore, Moreitti."

"Hey, can I help it that the ladies want a taste of me?" He smirked then winked down at me. "So, how about that shopping? What would you like? Any store in this joint, price doesn't matter."

I was going to get a headache from all the eye-rolling I was doing because of him. "You're an idiot, you know that, right?"

"Compared to you, Einstein was an idiot too, so your insult can't really hurt me, sweetheart." Putting his hand at the small of my back, he guided me away from the food court and toward the third-floor entrance into Nordstrom.

"Why are we going in here?" I complained, digging in my heels.

"Don't they have a little bit of everything? Figured we couldn't go wrong in here."

"Yeah, no." I grabbed his wrist and tugged him toward the escalators. "Do I look like I normally shop in places like that? No thanks. And besides, I'm not letting you buy something expensive. Not how I work, Moreitti."

"Anyone ever tell you that you are a pain in the ass?" he grumbled.

I grinned. "You're the first, actually."

Chapter 8
Braxton

I followed Barrick off the plane and into the airport. Some guy on his cell got in my way as we were on our way out, and I bared my teeth at him, not in the mood to be the least bit understanding when he should have been watching what he was doing in the first place.

My face must have shown just what kind of mood I was in, because the guy hastily got out of my way, muttering a quick apology. I saw Barrick glance at me out of the corner of my eye, but he stayed quiet even as I felt his concern.

I didn't sleep last night. Instead, I'd been trying to get the story of my engagement to Darcy taken down from all the sites that were gushing over the wedding and alleged baby we were having. Fucking hell, like I would subject a poor defenseless child to a mother like that bitch. Some people shouldn't ever have kids, and Darcy was definitely one of them.

It wasn't that I cared if the world thought I was going to marry her and we were starting a family. No, fuck them. I didn't give two shits what they thought because there was no way in hell it was happening. Ever.

It was Nevaeh I didn't want to have to see that trash all over social media and tabloids and fuck knows what else. Not until I could explain everything to her. In the past two years, we had become close. She was my best friend, and I'd confided a lot of my secrets in her.

But I'd never told her about Darcy and that I'd gotten engaged to her right out of high school. I didn't know how Neveah would take my one and only past relationship, or what she would think if she saw all the articles and social media posts about the bogus wedding and my allegedly impending fatherhood.

Earlier that morning, I'd decided I couldn't chance her finding out over the weekend and knew I needed to see her and explain. Barrick had jumped at the idea of going to California, and we were in the last two seats on a plane bound for LAX two hours later.

"Barrick!"

The sound of Mia's voice had both our heads snapping up. There, standing beside a blacked-out SUV, was Mia. She sprinted toward us. More than three feet away, she jumped, knowing Barrick would catch her. She wrapped her legs around his waist, and he kissed her like they hadn't seen each other in weeks instead of less than twenty-four hours.

"Is your leg okay?" he asked when he pulled back, one of his hands rubbing at her braced knee.

"It's fine. And now that you two are here, everything is perfect." She glanced over at me after kissing him again. "Hey, stranger."

Seeing her, some of the dark clouds hanging over my head dissipated. Nevaeh was my best friend, but Mia was a close second. I loved her like a sister, but I needed her just as much as I needed my little kitten.

Barrick placed her carefully on her feet, and she put her arm through mine, walking us toward her mother's vehicle where two large bodyguards were waiting. "I knew you wouldn't be able to stay away," she said quietly, her big green eyes sparkling with amusement.

"That's not why I'm here, Mia," I told her as we reached the SUV. Her mother was already sitting inside, her phone—which seemed to be permanently attached to her hand—out while she typed away one-handed and drank her coffee with the other. "My parents fucked me over last night."

Mia's eyes widened, and she turned to face me fully, concern on her face. "What happened?"

"Apparently Brax is getting a wife and a kid all in one," Barrick commented as he tossed his stuff in the back then walked around to where we were standing.

"What the hell are you talking about?" she demanded, putting her hands on her hips as she glared from him to me. "You aren't even dating anyone, and if you tell me you've been meeting some chick in secret while Nev has been—" She broke off, sucking in a deep breath. Sweat beaded on her upper lip, and I swear she turned green right before my eyes. "Fuck. Why does this shit happen when I get pissed?" she moaned.

Barrick wrapped his arms around her, pulling her head to his shoulder. "It's okay, firecracker. It will pass." He kissed the top of her head. "Have you been sick all day?"

She nodded, leaning against him weakly.

"You should have stayed home," he muttered. "I told you I don't like you traveling without me when you're—"

"Pregnant," I blurted out, realization hitting me dead center. "You're pregnant?"

"Apparently," she groaned and bent in half to vomit at our feet.

"Damn, again?" Emmie Armstrong stuck her head out of the SUV. "Ah, baby girl. Let's get you home. You need to rest. Momma will make you something to help with the nausea."

Once Mia was done puking, Barrick picked her up and put her in the back seat beside her mom. She cuddled up to the woman who looked like an older version of her and closed her eyes. "This sucks so bad," she mumbled.

"I know, honey. Believe me, I know." Emmie stroked her hair as we got in. Once we were settled and the guard behind the wheel pulled into traffic, she glanced at me. "Did I hear you're going to be a father, too?"

"No, ma'am," I told her. "Not happening. I wouldn't trust that bitch with a dog, let alone make her a mother."

"I don't understand," she said, her eyes narrowing.

"It's a long story," Barrick said with a sigh. "But basically, his parents set him up last night. They announced to everyone they knew would spread the news like wildfire that he was marrying his high school girlfriend, and when he tried to tell everyone the truth, she put the nail in the coffin by announcing that she is pregnant."

"So, you're not getting married, and there is no baby?" she asked for clarification.

"Fuck no to both," I bit out. "Ma'am."

She grinned at me. "Okay, then. Well, I'll take care of it. Don't worry."

"I don't care what the hell they say or do. It's not happening. I just don't want Nevaeh to get upset," I told her honestly.

She pressed her lips together for a moment, then shrugged. "That, I can't promise. I mean, Nevaeh is kind of fragile right now with her dad's illness, and I can never determine what that girl will do when she's not herself. Okay, scratch that. I can't figure her out on the best of days, let alone when she's upset. But I can deal with the media and get the story squashed if you want. And I can also deal with the parentals and the ex."

"Thanks, Momma," Mia told her weakly. "I knew you would help."

"Anything to make it easier on you, my baby." Emmie kissed her forehead and gave me a wink. "Braxton is family. Something you should know by now, kid. I take care of my family."

For some reason, knowing she was going to help me out of this mess made something burn in my chest. In the two years Mia had been in my life, her family had made me feel more a part of their inner world than my own parents ever had. They included me in everything, from Christmas to getting cards and text messages on my birthday. Emmie and her husband even invited me to their house during summer breaks when Mia flew home for a few weeks.

It wasn't just the Armstrongs. Nevaeh's parents were just as welcoming and accepting as Mia's. Maybe more so. When Nevaeh was away at school, they texted me at least once a week. It was initially to check in on her and get an honest answer. But they would always include me in their texts, asking how I was and even inquiring on how Sasha was doing. Then, I got the weekly texts even when Nevaeh wasn't in Virginia. More often than not, it was Lana Stevenson, and I could feel the maternal concern she had for me even three thousand miles away. But Drake would text me from time to time too, separately from his wife.

Now, however, I wondered if things were going to be different with them. I wanted to be with Nev—*would* fucking be with her—and even if they didn't like it, she was going to be mine.

Chapter 9
Braxton

Because I wanted to surprise Nevaeh, we went back to Mia's parents' house instead of going to Nevaeh's, even though I was itching to see her again. When I realized I had a few texts from her, I replied back, pretending like I was busy and that I would call her later that night so I could tell her happy birthday.

Mia spent the rest of the afternoon in her room resting after her mom made her some kind of lemony concoction she said worked wonders for morning sickness. Whatever it was seemed to help because Barrick told us she passed out after she finally got comfortable and was sleeping peacefully.

That Mia was pregnant freaked me out a little. I didn't like seeing her sick or hurting in any shape or form. She had life growing inside of her, a new member of my family, and I was already praying it was a boy because I didn't know how either Barrick or I were going to keep up with all the dead bodies we would have to hide once a girl started getting noticed by boys. Because if it was a girl, and she looked like her mother, they would be noticing early, and I didn't think Virginia was big enough for all the bastards I would need to bury for touching Uncle Braxton's precious baby.

I told Barrick that, and his face turned just as green as Mia's had earlier. "Same, bro. Same."

Emmie laughed as she listened to us while she made us each a sandwich in the kitchen. "You two are adorable, but fuck, you make my heart so damn happy that you're Mia's."

"I would love a daughter. A little version of Mia running around, making my life difficult and complete, with red pigtails bouncing all over the place. I'd be okay with that," Barrick said, his eyes widening at the truth of his own admission. "But I think I would be a basket case from the second she's born."

"Oh, I know you would be," she assured him with a grin. "That is what is going to make you a great father, Barrick. Don't worry, you'll get used to that feeling of panic when you think of your children. Trust me, it never goes away. It just gets easier to accept as reality." She twisted her lips and placed his plate in front of him. "Or you hire some retired Marine security heir to watch over her, they fall in love, and you start to breathe a small fraction easier."

"You know many of those fuckers?" he asked with a wry grin.

Sighing heavily, she shoved at the back of his head playfully. "I know many people, from every walk of life. Lucky for you, I didn't have to ask for a favor and make you disappear."

Even though she was still grinning, I knew in my gut she wasn't joking. I likened Emmie to a mob boss with how easily she could get things "taken care of." I'd thought my cousin Lyla was the most badass woman I'd ever met until I met Mia's mom. I possessed equal parts respect for and fear of the little redhead with big green eyes that looked so much like her daughter, I couldn't help but love the woman.

After we ate, I showered in the guest room that had become my regular room when I visited.

The house Mia grew up in wasn't the mansion I'd called home the first eighteen years of my life, but it wasn't a shack. It was the largest house on her block, with six bedrooms, right on the beach. There was a guesthouse out back where the two bodyguards stayed when they weren't escorting Mia's mother or another member of her family. But the biggest difference was that this house was full of warmth and love that hit a person direct center as soon as they stepped across the threshold.

By the time Mia woke from her nap, her father and brother were home from golfing, and we left soon after for the party. The Armstrongs lived in Malibu, but Nevaeh's house was in Santa Monica. We all piled into Emmie's SUV, minus the bodyguards, and made the drive over.

There were already vehicles everywhere when we pulled up. The driveway was overflowing, and people had parked on the street, all of them there for Nevaeh's birthday party. Climbing out of the back, I double-checked that the present I'd brought for her was still in my pocket and then followed everyone to the house.

Emmie rang the doorbell, and only a moment later, the door swung open. One of Jesse Thornton's twin sons answered the door. Luca and Lyric were identical, and in the past, the only way I'd been able to determine who was who was that Luca seemed to have Shane Stevenson's daughter by his side at all times. Then they had started inking their bodies right after their eighteenth birthday, so I'd been able to tell which one was which easier.

"Welcome," Luca greeted, smirking at his aunt, the sleeve of ink on his left arm telling me which twin he was. "Come in, if you dare."

"Fuck," Nik muttered. "What have you done this time?"

Luca's expression turned wounded, but there was amusement shining out of his eyes that constantly changed from one shade of brown to another. "That hurts, Uncle Nik. Really, you hit me right in the feels, man."

"Yeah, whatever. Now what did you do?"

Luca's answer was to wink and step back, waving us in. "The birthday girl isn't here yet. Guess it's cool to be late to your own party. I mean, I didn't even show up to mine, so whatevs."

"No, he was too busy getting in Megan Hawthorn's pants to care he had people waiting to wish him happy birthday," a voice that was so sweet I almost missed the bite to it said.

I glanced over Luca's shoulder to see the girl he was normally with shoot daggers at his back as she walked by. He clenched his jaw, muttered something under his breath I didn't hear, and shut the front door with unneeded force, causing his father to shoot him a hard glare.

"Excuse me while I go set the record straight. Again," he said before turning and following Violet Stevenson. "It only makes the two hundredth time."

"That girl can make that boy sweat without even trying," Nik said with a deep chuckle as we walked farther into the house.

Halfway across the living room, I caught sight of Nevaeh's mom, and she quickly left the group she was talking to. She hugged me tightly. "This is the best surprise," she said as she pulled back, a beaming smile on her beautiful face. "Nev is going to be so happy you made it."

"Where is she?" I asked before I could stop myself, needing to see her, touch her.

"That is a good question. She was supposed to be home by now, but knowing Jordan, it's hard to tell what kind of trouble those two got into." She grimaced. "If she doesn't get home soon, I'm sending out the big guns."

"Aunt Gabs is here?" Mia asked as she glanced around.

Lana shook her head. "Not yet. She and Liam are on their way, though. Or so he told Drake about fifteen minutes ago. If she gets here and Jordan hasn't shown up, I'm going to sic her on him."

I barely paid their conversation any attention. Jealousy was eating through me, and I was two seconds away from pulling out a few big guns of my own. Mia's best friend visited us every few weeks. I liked him… Until he flirted with Nevaeh. Then I wanted to rip his arms off his body and beat the living hell out of him with them.

Now she was out with him, doing fuck knew what. She was legal now, could do anything she wanted, with whomever she wanted.

"There you are," a deep voice said from behind me. "Do you realize how hard it is to find you, woman?"

Turning, I saw Jordan coming toward us, with no Nevaeh in sight. He walked up to Mia, threw an arm around her shoulders, and kissed the top of her head. Barrick clenched his jaw but didn't say anything about it. He was used to their relationship and trusted Mia, but I knew just how jealous he was right then. That same jealousy burned through me whenever the guy so casually did the same with Nevaeh.

"There's this thing called a phone," Mia sassed him. "You use it to call, text, even send social media messages. It's all the rage these days. Maybe you should try it."

"Yeah, but then I wouldn't get to see your beautiful face, and that really should be considered a crime."

"Um, excuse you," Lana said with a mock glare at him. "You should have had my child home half an hour ago at the latest. Where is she?"

"Sorry, we lost track of time. She's changing now."

"Perfect." She touched my arm, then pushed me. "You should go help her with her zipper," she suggested with a grin. "She had the worst time with it when she was trying it on at the mall earlier."

***

The first time I'd ever set eyes on Nevaeh, my heart had stopped.

I was sitting on the couch with Sasha beside me, and Mia answered the Skype call from her cousin. Her beautiful face appeared on the laptop screen, and even as she was yelling at her sister, I'd felt something wake up inside me for the first time in my life.

It was like she'd hit pause on my heart because it didn't beat, while other parts of my body came alive for the first time since I'd lost my leg. She'd blinked, her blue-gray eyes looking huge behind her glasses, like some animated kitten about to pounce on her unsuspecting prey.

Then she'd started vomiting words she hadn't wanted to utter but was helpless not to, and it was so adorable, I found myself laughing. In that moment, with her beautiful face flushing with the most adorable shade of pink and her dropping her head into her hands, I knew.

She was mine.

Then Mia had dropped the biggest, most painful bomb in my lap. The helpless feeling I got when she said Nevaeh wasn't even sixteen yet was worse than when I lost my leg. I felt sick to my soul, because I'd instantly wanted her and knew I couldn't have her.

Then I'd met her in person, and I fought my feelings tooth and nail. I ached for days after, wanting her. Just to hold her, touch my fingers to her baby-soft cheek, brush my lips over her plump lips, and inhale the scent of her skin. I knew if I saw her again—fuck, if I just heard her voice again—I would be lost completely. It was why I'd practically begged Mia to talk her cousin out of attending school with us. I needed distance, as much as humanly possible, to keep my sanity, to protect her from all the thoughts I had rioting through my head on a marathon loop of all the things I wanted to do to and with her.

And then I found out about what happened after I left her in New York, and I couldn't breathe. I didn't know exactly what had gone down—not until she told me months later—but I knew something had upset her. Someone scared her, took something from her they had no business taking, and I wanted to break his fucking neck.

I couldn't stay away after that. Couldn't get past wanting to protect her from everything life could throw at her, my sweet little kitten who never should have to know the dangers of the outside world. As long as I could be beside her, I would find the strength to hold my feelings in check.

Just until her eighteenth birthday.

As I walked up the stairs to her bedroom, I felt my heart jackhammering in my chest. I was moments away from seeing her, and now I didn't have to hold back. I could hold her, touch her, kiss and taste her all I wanted. I had two years of wanting, aching, and craving her to catch up on, and I was going to get my fill.

Stopping outside her bedroom door, I inhaled deeply and slowly let it out as I lifted my hand and knocked.

"Just a sec," she called out, and I braced myself by putting my hands on either side of the doorframe.

Closing my eyes, I waited, blocking out the sounds of the party from below so I could savor every moment of seeing her. I heard the doorknob turn and felt the air shift as it swung inward. Her soft gasp had my eyes snapping open, and I took in all of her slowly.

Her feet were bare, as were her legs. I lifted my gaze hungrily, pausing at the hem of her dress that started mid-thigh. Up and up I went, past the flare of her hips, over her flat stomach and her perfect tits. Her hair fell over her left shoulder as she stood there with her hands lifted to fasten an earring in her right ear. There was no makeup to enhance her angel-like beauty, and even though she wasn't wearing her glasses, her blue-gray eyes still had that animated kitten quality to them as she blinked at me in utter surprise.

"Braxton," she whispered, her chest heaving as she met my hungry gaze.

"You're so goddamn beautiful, baby," I rasped, my voice full of the need that had been gnawing at me for years.

Nevaeh instinctively took a step back, and then another, until I was inside her bedroom and was able to close the door. Then I grabbed her hips, my fingers biting desperately into her flesh through the material of her dress as I swung her around and pressed her against the door.

"Brax," she moaned, her back arching, pressing her chest into mine as I lowered my head slowly until my breath was bathing her plump lips. "Please."

"Tell me what you want, Kitten," I commanded, brushing my nose over hers. "I need to hear you say it."

"Kiss me," she begged. "Please, just one kiss. P-please."

Her voice broke on the last plea, and I couldn't have held back another second even if our lives depended on it. Cupping the back of her skull in one hand, I tilted her head so I could take as much of her mouth as I wanted while my lips sealed to hers. Her fingers twisted in my black button-up, pulling me impossibly closer as she sighed into my mouth.

I swallowed it, then thrust my tongue deep, tasting every inch of her sweetness. I felt more than heard her moan and pressed her harder against the door.

When I lifted my head an indeterminate period later, we were both gasping for breath, and her mouth looked as though I'd ravished it. Panting heavily, she rubbed her thighs together unconsciously, and it took every ounce of self-control I had left not to carry her to her bed and spread her open for me so I could taste her pussy and relieve the ache she felt that was making her squirm against me.

Instead, I cupped her chin and angled her head so she was forced to meet my gaze. "Happy birthday, Kitten."

Chapter 10
Nevaeh

I could still feel his lips imprinted on mine. Every time I licked my lips, I tasted him, no matter what I drank or ate.

After that amazing, bone-melting kiss—the first kiss I should have had and not the one Dax had forced on me years before—he'd helped me zip up my dress then taken my hand. Kissing my knuckles, he'd opened the door he'd just had me pressed up against and walked me downstairs.

My legs had still been shaky, so I was glad to have him to guide me because I knew I never would have made it down on my own. My family and loved ones surrounded us the instant we reached the first floor, and he stayed beside me over the next two hours. Putting drink after drink in my hand, feeding me from the plate Mom pushed into his hands at one point, loaded with all my favorite finger foods.

I heard every word people said to me, but then I would look into Braxton's hungry eyes, and I would forget what we were talking about. Sly grins were tossed our way, but I didn't see a single one of them. My focus was drawn over and over again to the man at my side, and I couldn't bring myself to care that everyone in my parents' house was there to wish me a happy birthday.

All I wanted was to be alone with Brax. I wished we were back in Virginia, just the two of us alone in the house, and that he would do more than just kiss me breathless. I wanted to know what the rest of him tasted like, not just his delicious mouth.

And then Daddy put his arm around my shoulders, and I was pulled back into reality. I'd seen him walking around talking to all our guests, laughing and joking with everyone, and every time, a feeling of the most acute sadness would make me feel like I was drowning in unshed tears. Every time, Braxton would see them and rub his thumb over my bottom lip, whisper, "Kitten," and make me forget about the pain wanting to consume me.

But with Daddy now holding me against his side as he lifted his glass of clear soda to toast me, his firstborn and his second angel, the tears won out. Not even Braxton's soothing touch could stop them from flooding down my face or the sob that was already bubbling in my chest from escaping.

I turned my face into Daddy's chest and inhaled deeply, memorizing his scent, what it felt like to have his arms around me, how safe and loved I was when he was this close, and I made a birthday wish for the first time since I was a little girl and still believed in wishes.

I wish for thirty, forty… No! I wish for fifty more years of this.

The sob finally escaped, and I amended my wish because I knew I was being too greedy.

Please. Just one more year of this. That's all I want. Just one more birthday of getting my daddy's hugs and him whispering how proud he is of me and how much he loves me. One. More. Year.

I felt his lips brushing over the top of my head and heard him begging me not to cry, and I quickly swallowed the rest of the sob trying to destroy this perfect night with him and the rest of my family. While I tried to control myself, I heard him whispering something to Braxton. Through my tears, I saw Brax nod.

The next thing I knew, I was outside, the cool air kissing my skin and making the tears on my cheeks feel like ice as Braxton carried me to Aunt Emmie's SUV. I was deposited in the back seat while Barrick and Mia got into the front, and Barrick started the vehicle.

"I-I'm sorry," I told them. "D-did I ruin the party?"

"No, Kitten," Braxton said as he pressed his lips to my temple and stroked his fingers through my tangled hair. "Your dad just wanted you to get some fresh air."

"But…" I glanced out the window of the SUV and felt my heart clench painfully as we drove away from my parents' house. "Why are we leaving, then?"

"It was either leave or start hiding bodies," Barrick said from the driver's seat as he carefully drove through my old neighborhood and then past Uncle Shane's and Uncle Axton's houses.

I furrowed my brow, confused, and Mia, who was turned in the front passenger seat watching me with pained eyes, gave me a tiny smile. "Braxton was about to piss on you to mark his territory. Jagger and Cannon were being their normal selves, flirting with you. Nothing serious, but I feared for my brother's life. Then Jordan was making comments about how hot you were now that you're legal. And when you started crying, all three were trying to hug you. It was when Brax started literally growling that we figured it was time to put some distance between you and every other non-blood-related male in a fifty-mile radius. Momma agreed and threw Barrick the keys."

"Oh," I murmured, sniffling indelicately.

Even after our kiss earlier, it was hard to wrap my head around the change in Braxton's and my relationship. I'd spent the past two years wanting him in a way I still didn't fully understand, thinking he wouldn't ever want me with the same desperation I felt. Now he was sitting in the back seat of a darkened SUV with me on his lap, his hands in my hair, and his nose pressed to my neck as he inhaled my scent like he'd been denied oxygen and I was the life-giving air he needed to survive.

I'd been so happy and lost in the feeling of having Braxton's complete attention that I hadn't given anyone else much mind. Jagger and Cannon flirting with me was nothing unusual. I was used to the two of them making asses of themselves over Arella and me. I took Jordan about as seriously as I did those two clowns, which was not at all.

Admittedly, I'd had a good time with Jordan that afternoon. He was funny, and when he wasn't being a horndog, salivating over anything with a vagina and breasts, he was kind of sweet. He didn't even blink when I bought an entire basket full of books in the bookstore, and he carried the three bags to his car like I hadn't just made him spend three hundred dollars on books he would never have thought would make for enjoyable entertainment. But he didn't call me a freak for liking to read things no one else would ever want to.

But even as I was laughing with him while we drank milk shakes near the beach not far from my house, I'd been missing Braxton.

"Where am I going, firecracker?" I heard Barrick ask Mia quietly.

"Nevaeh, honey, do you want to go anywhere?" Reaching back, she clasped my hand and gave it a gentle squeeze. "Or we could just drive around for a little while until you feel better and Brax has calmed down."

My skin erupted in goose bumps when Braxton gave my shoulder an openmouthed kiss. I arched my neck, giving him better access. I wanted more of those kinds of kisses all over my body. "Just drive,"

I told her, and she quickly turned around, telling Barrick which way to turn so we could get on PCH.

Pushing my hair out of his way, Braxton kissed a hot trail down my shoulder then over the part of my back that was exposed by my dress. I bit my lip, but it didn't keep the mewling sounds I was helpless to hold in from escaping.

"You're killing me, Kitten," he murmured against the shell of my ear. "Feel what you do to me?"

I squirmed on his lap, feeling the hard evidence of his need for me pulsing against my thigh. I wrapped my arms around his neck and laid my head on his shoulder, looking up at him through my lashes, and I shifted my hips until he was nestled against my ass through his jeans.

"Fuck," he groaned, and I watched his beautiful, masculine mouth form the word.

Suddenly, the music was turned on, the volume up as loud as it would go. The bass of the song vibrated through the entire vehicle, making the windows shake, but I was thankful for the loudness to drown out the sounds that came from my throat when Braxton turned me on his lap so I was straddling him. When I sat on his lap like that, my dress rode up, exposing my panties to him as he cupped my ass and pressed my core down onto his hard-on.

Neither of us moved, just stared at each other as I sat there, my panties soaked through as he let me feel his reaction to me. I should have been embarrassed, letting him look at me, feel how wet I was for him while Mia and Barrick sat so close. But it wasn't like they'd never made out in front of me before.

His fingers clenched and released, massaging my flesh through my panties and making me so wet, my thighs became saturated with it.

I began to tremble with all the suppressed need that had been building deep inside me, and my fingers shook as I started unbuttoning his shirt, needing to touch his skin. He groaned when I had it undone and pulled free from his jeans, his chest and hard stomach on full display to my gaze. It was dark out and the moon was hiding behind a bank of clouds, but streetlights and oncoming cars' headlights gave me plenty of light to see him.

I memorized the feel of his skin, the sharp ridges and angles of his tight abs. His body heat burned my fingertips. I'd seen the ink on his chest so often, I knew exactly where every piece of artwork was, and I traced each one with my fingernails.

One of his hands left my ass and caught mine, guiding it down to the buckle of his belt. Our gazes locked as I undid it along with the snap of his jeans. I carefully lowered the zipper. But when my fingers found the band of his boxer briefs, I hesitated, nervousness hitting me for the first time.

I wanted to touch that part of him, wanted to know what it felt like—what it would taste like. This was one of those many, many firsts I'd been dreaming of having with Braxton.

Sensing my hesitation, he cupped my face in both his hands, rubbing his thumbs over my lips as his dark eyes asked me what was wrong. Swallowing hard, I shook my head, unable to find the words to tell him what was in my head. And my heart.

Pulling my head down to his, he brushed his lips over my neck on his way to my ear. "I'm sorry, baby. I'm rushing you, and there's no need for that," he said just loud enough for me to hear him over the music. "We have all the time in the world, Kitten. Forever."

I closed my eyes as I let that one word float over my entire body, soothing something I didn't know needed to be soothed. With one hand, he cupped the back of my head, the other rubbing down my spine. It didn't calm the raging need pulsing through me, making my panties and thighs wetter and wetter with every breath I took. It only made my heart ache more because in that moment, I felt cherished and precious to him.

Chapter 11
Nevaeh

It was late by the time Barrick pulled Aunt Emmie's SUV into my parents' driveway. Braxton opened the door and stepped out before reaching in to help me down. As soon as my feet were on the ground, I wrapped my arms around his waist and breathed in deeply.

Combing his fingers through my hair, he tilted my head back and kissed the tip of my nose. "I'll meet you at the airport."

"Okay," I whispered, already missing him. PopPop's jet had an early takeoff time scheduled, so it was only going to be a few hours until I saw him again, but I didn't want to leave him.

With another kiss, he walked me up to the porch and waited until I unlocked the door before turning to go. Swallowing hard, I slowly walked through the house to the kitchen to get a bottle of water before going to bed.

Pushing open the door, I stopped when I saw Daddy sitting at the kitchen table. I stopped mid-step and sucked in a deep breath. His long, dark hair was sprinkled with strands of gray, his blue-gray eyes full of worry.

Giving me a grim smile, he lifted his mug of tea. "Want some? It's ginger to help with my nausea."

I tried to smile back, but from the way his lips pressed together, I didn't think I pulled it off. "Sure," I choked out.

Standing, he walked to the stove where the teakettle was resting. Placing a tea bag in a mug, he added the hot water and grabbed the honey and a spoon on his way back to the table where I'd sat down.

Placing everything in front of me, he retook his seat. I added the honey, keeping my gaze on my mug so I didn't have to look at him, knowing if I did, I would start crying all over again.

"It's okay to be scared, Nevaeh. It's even okay to be angry."

I lifted startled eyes and finally looked at him. "Who would I be angry at?"

"Me," he said with a shrug. "I did this. It's my fault I'm sick right now. You're allowed to be pissed at me for doing this to you and your mom."

Reaching out, I wrapped my fingers around his hand, shivering when I felt how cold it was. "Daddy, I'm not mad. Not at you, never you. I know you had a drinking problem before you met Mom. You never talk about why you became an alcoholic, and I won't make you tell me, but I realize it must have been bad."

His jaw clenched, and I saw his Adam's apple bob several times before he nodded. "Yeah, sweetheart. It was bad. I won't put those nightmares in your head, but the booze kept me numb. I liked that feeling a hell of a lot. Until the drinking cost me your mom. She's why I stopped, why I haven't picked up a bottle in over twenty years." He closed his eyes and lowered his head. "And now, the consequences of all that heavy drinking could take everything away."

"Daddy—"

His eyes snapped open, and when I saw the tears in his eyes, my own burned and filled. "It's okay to be scared and angry, because I'm terrified and so fucking pissed at myself, I can't breathe at times. I'm sorry, honey. So damn sorry that I might be taken away from you and your mother. I love you. More than anything, I love you."

"I-I love you too, Daddy," I told him around the lump that was choking me. "And you're right, I am scared. Nothing has ever scared me as much as the thought of losing you."

"I'm going to do everything I can not to let that happen, Nev." Tugging on my hand, he pulled me up and onto his lap. Like this, I felt like I was a little girl again, but having Daddy hold me and press a kiss to my temple was the best feeling in the world. My tears spilled over my lashes, and he wiped them away. "Leaving you and our family behind is the last thing I want to do. But…" I fought back a sob, already knowing what he was going to say. "But we have to face reality, sweetheart. This operation might not work. I could reject the liver, or it could fail, or any number of things could go wrong."

"I know," I whispered.

"If any of those things happens and I'm no longer here, I need you to know how much I love you and your brother and sisters. How proud you've made me." Tears were pouring out of his eyes now, but he gave me a brave smile. "Nothing has made me happier than getting to be your dad. You and your mom have given me an amazing life. The things that came before you and her…they no longer matter. I've had perfection with my family, and I'll never take any of those years for granted."

"Daddy, you're talking like you expect to die." I threw my arms around him, my shoulders shaking as I fought not to break down completely. I needed to be strong—for him, if no other reason. "You can't die, Daddy. You can't! Please, please don't leave me."

"I can't promise that, Nev. I wish I could, but I won't lie to you." He wrapped his arms around me, squeezing me gently. "All I can promise is that you will be okay. None of you will ever have to worry about anything. Ever."

"I don't care about that!" I couldn't hold on a second longer. The sobs left me, making my entire body quake and ache from the force of them. "Money means nothing. Having material things is useless to me. None of it matters if you're not here."

"I know, sweetheart." He rocked me in his arms, kissing the top of my head. "It's okay. Everything is going to be okay."

I could only hope he was right.

***

My eyes still felt swollen when I got on the plane the next morning. I'd cried all night until my throat was aching and my voice was hoarse.

I didn't want to go back to Virginia, wanting to stay so I could have as much time with Daddy as possible before his surgery, which had been scheduled for the week before Christmas, but he wouldn't let me. The semester was almost over, with only finals to deal with before I came back for the holiday break, and he refused to let me put my education on hold.

Sunglasses perched on my nose instead of my normal prescription glasses, I didn't look at anyone as I dropped down into one of the seats and fastened the belt. The flight attendant asked me if I wanted anything to drink, but I just turned my gaze out the window, unable to answer her without crying again.

Braxton's warm hand covered mine, and I sucked in a shuddery breath, fighting the tears that wanted to be released. "What can I do?" he asked quietly, his thumb stroking over my knuckles.

My chin trembled, but I kept my eyes trained on the window without seeing anything outside. "Just hold me," I whispered brokenly.

"Always, Kitten," he said reverently as he unfastened my belt and pulled me onto his lap. I laid my head on his chest and let the tears leak from my eyes the entire flight back to Virginia.

Chapter 12
Braxton

With Nevaeh's head pressed against my chest, I carried her into her room and laid her on her bed. The whole flight home, she'd done nothing but cry silently, then on the drive from the airport, she'd fallen asleep against me.

Pulling back the covers, I took off her shoes then tucked the thick comforter around her, taking off her glasses and putting them on the nightstand. She sighed softly and folded her hands under her cheek as she turned onto her side. As I looked down at her, my heart clenched painfully, seeing the tear tracks on her beautiful face that was pale from exhaustion and grief.

Bending, I brushed my lips over her cheek and would have left her to rest, but when I straightened, she caught my fingers with her hand. Surprised, I looked down to find her wide awake, her swollen eyes blinking up at me. For the longest time, we just gazed at each other, and then she gave a weak tug on my fingers.

"Don't go," she pleaded in a voice that sounded painfully hoarse from all the crying she'd done.

"Are you sure?" I asked, even though my first instinct was to give her exactly what she wanted and crawl into bed beside her. "You need to rest, Kitten."

"I need you to hold me," she said weakly, her chin trembling. "P-please?"

"Ah, baby, you don't have to beg. I'll give you anything you want, no matter what it is." Kicking off my shoes, I carefully climbed in beside her, positioning us so I was lying on the side with my good leg.

As soon as I was beside her, she wrapped herself around me. It was so natural, it was like she'd been doing it forever. She fit so perfectly against me it was as if we'd both been created to fit each other.

With her head on my shoulder and her arms around my waist, I wrapped my arms around her and kissed the top of her head.

"What about Sasha?" she whispered after a few minutes passed.

"She's staying with Lyla and Howler. She will be okay for another night. We can pick her up in the morning." Brushing her hair back from her face, I rubbed my thumb over her cheek. "You should sleep, baby. You need to rest."

"I can't," she murmured. "All I can think about is Daddy. I wish I were back there with him right now, Brax. What… What if something happens to him and I'm here?"

The thought of her back in California without me made my heart pound. I didn't want to be away from her. But I knew she needed to be closer with how sick her dad was. "Don't think about the negative," I told her, trying to hide the fact that I was already clawing at the walls of my sanity just thinking of her being so far away without me. "Mia's mom said he has the best doctors, and we'll be back in a few weeks for Christmas and winter break. Once he has his surgery, he will be good as new."

"Y-you think so?" There was so much hope in her voice, it broke my heart.

"Yeah, Kitten. I really do." I lifted her chin with my thumb. "Would I ever lie to you?"

She shook her head. "Never."

"And I never will," I promised. "Your dad is going to be okay, baby."

"You have more faith in that than he seems to," she said sadly. "He wants me to prepare myself in case something does happen to him. I don't know what I'll do if we lose him, Brax. I can't picture my life without him in it. Just thinking about it, I feel like there's this gaping hole in the middle of my chest, trying to suck all the happiness out of the world and into some black void where I can't smile. I can't breathe for the pressure it puts on my lungs."

"Don't think about that. For now, just concentrate on your finals and Christmas shopping." I rubbed one hand down her back before cupping her ass. Giving it a firm squeeze, I pressed my lower half into her. "Think about this, Kitten. And how good I'm going to make you feel."

She let out a little mewling sound that went straight to my cock, making it twitch against her. "Brax."

"Now that you're eighteen, we don't have to hold back. I can kiss you and touch you and hold you as much as you'll let me." I kissed the corner of her mouth, causing her to gasp in pleasure.

"I never wanted you to hold back," she moaned. "I've craved you, Braxton. Your kisses, your touch, your arms around me every night. But I thought you didn't want me."

I skimmed my nose down her neck, inhaling her scent and causing her to shiver. "I'm sorry, baby. I didn't mean for you to think I didn't want you. I was just trying to keep myself in check so I didn't fuck this up for us."

Her fingers combed through the short hair at the back of my neck, holding me to her. "I want you so much right now…but, could I have a shower first?" she asked shyly.

I lifted my head. Seeing how pink her cheeks were, guilt filled me. "If I'm going too fast for you, let me know. I'll slow down for you, Nev. Just say the word, and I'll give you whatever you need."

"You're not going too fast," she said with a tiny smile. "If anything, I think this is long overdue. But I need a girl moment. Give me half an hour, tops. I want everything to be perfect."

"Then take all the time you need." Sitting up in her bed, I leaned back against the headboard. She jumped to her feet then paused on her walk to her bathroom, glancing at me over her shoulder. "You'll still be here when I get back, right?"

"I'm going to grab a quick shower in my room, but I'll be right here when you come out," I promised with a grin. "Go, Nev, before I decide to join you in there. I'm not sure you're ready for that yet."

With a yelp, she ran into the bathroom, locking the door behind her. Laughing softly to myself, I waited until I heard the shower turn on before getting to my feet. I walked out of her room just as Mia was coming down the hall toward her and Barrick's room.

"She okay?" Mia asked, her face pinched with concern for her cousin.

"She's showering now," I told her evasively.

"I called her parents to let them know we made it back okay." She grimaced, turning green. It was a color that was becoming a normal shade for her face. "I think I'm going to go take a nap. Don't wake me up for dinner."

"Got it. Get some rest. I'll take care of Nevaeh," I assured her.

A sly grin teased at her lips. "I bet you will." But then the grin turned serious. "You need to tell her about the whole Darcy thing."

"I will," I muttered, not wanting to get into the whole situation with my parents and ex yet.

"Soon, Brax," she warned.

"I said I will, Mia," I told her frustratedly, scrubbing a hand over my face. I needed to shave the scruff off my jaw so I didn't scratch Nevaeh.

"I just don't want you to leave it too long. Nev is really vulnerable right now. This crap with your family and that Darcy bitch could end badly. I don't want Nev to get hurt when she doesn't have to be."

I blew out a tired sigh, knowing she was right. "I'll do it soon, I promise. Just not today, okay? We have other things we need to figure out before I bring up that bullshit."

She nodded. "Yeah, okay. I'll let you figure it out on your own." Walking around me, she opened her bedroom door, and moments later, I thought I heard her moan of contentment.

This pregnancy was wearing her down already, and I hoped the whole morning sickness thing didn't last long. I hated seeing her unwell. It made me feel helpless because there was nothing I could do to make it better for her. Just like I couldn't do anything to take away the pain and heartache Nevaeh was feeling over her dad.

Groaning, I went to my room. After shaving, I took a quick shower and was back in Nevaeh's room before she even turned off her own shower. Sitting on the edge of her bed, I sat there waiting as nervousness swamped me for the first time.

I hadn't had sex since the accident that had cost me my leg. Fuck, until I saw Nevaeh, it was like my dick didn't care if it ever saw any action again. From the first moment I set eyes on her, however, it had been paying just as much attention to her as my damn heart had.

Now that I was about to get the girl I'd been craving for over two years, my hands were sweating like it was my first time. Part of me wished it were. That this moment with Nevaeh was my first experience, because I fucking knew she was the one for me.

From the bathroom, I heard the water turn off, and my cock throbbed, tenting the material of the basketball shorts I'd pulled on after my shower. A short time later, the door opened, and she walked out, wrapped in nothing but a damp towel she clutched to her body like a shield.

All my nervousness evaporated, replaced by all the need and hunger I'd been unable to release because I wanted to make sure this thing between us was done right. Her long dark hair was still slightly wet and hung down her back in sexy waves. Her blue-gray eyes blinked at me, reminding me yet again of a curious little kitten as her gaze went straight to my bare chest and skimmed over my ink.

Standing, I walked toward her, not in the least bit self-conscious about the prosthesis showing under the shorts I was wearing. Nevaeh had never made me feel less for having lost my leg. It was like she didn't even see my disability, and that was only one of the thousands of things I loved about her.

As I neared, I saw the pink in her cheeks travel down her neck, across her chest, and over the tops of her breasts that were barely contained by the towel. "You are so damn beautiful, Kitten," I rasped, reaching her.

Tilting her chin up with my thumb, I let everything I was feeling for her shine out of my eyes as I lowered my head to brush my lips over hers. I felt her tremble against me for a moment before she released the hold she had on the towel and kissed me back.

She tasted of mint and something addictively sweet, and I ravished her mouth until we were both gasping for our next breaths. Dazedly, she clung to my shoulders as I lifted my head to gaze down at her nakedness. I'd never thought of any one person as perfect, but everything about Nevaeh was just that. She was pure perfection, every single inch of her calling to me to caress, kiss, and brand her as mine.

Stepping back, I offered her my hand. Biting her lip, she placed hers in mine, and I backed toward her bed, pulling her with me. "Are you sure this is what you want?" I asked her.

"More than anything," she whispered. "I want you so much, Brax. I need you."

I jerked her against me, unable to stand the distance between us a second longer. "Baby, I need you too. So fucking much, I can't think straight."

She smiled as she stroked the backs of her fingers down my jaw. "Then stop thinking, Braxton. Make me yours."

Chapter 13
Nevaeh

Rough hands caught me by the hips and lifted me off my feet. On instinct, my legs wrapped around his waist, and I held on as he dropped down on the edge of the bed. "You are mine, Kitten. You always have been. From the first time I saw you blinking back at me on that damn Skype call."

I pressed my hips down harder on his, only to have my breath catch when I felt his cock flex against my core. "Have you been mine too?"

His brow furrowed at my shy question. "You doubt it?"

"I…don't know," I answered honestly. "Please, just tell me."

"Every second, baby. I have belonged to you in every way." He cupped my face in hands that openly trembled, his callused thumbs rubbing over my cheeks tenderly. "I love you, Nevaeh Joy Stevenson."

Tears instantly filled my eyes. I knew he wanted me, could feel just how much pulsing against my core right then, but to have him confess he loved me… It was surreal and earthshaking. "Brax," I choked out, unable to hold back telling him exactly how I felt in return. "I love you too."

"Baby," he groaned, tipping my head back to meet his kiss.

The kiss didn't last more than a few seconds before his lips released mine. Need blazed out of his dark eyes as he cupped both of my breasts in his hands, his thumbs rubbing back and forth over my diamond-hard nipples.

"I've dreamed of these," he muttered. "I should be shot for all the things I've wanted to do to them."

"Tell me."

But he shook his head. "Not yet, baby. Soon, I'll show you. But right now, I'm going to make love to you, not fuck you like an animal."

Something deep inside me clenched, hard, and I felt my core gush. He must have felt the rush of wetness too, because he cursed almost violently, and suddenly, I was on my back and his face was buried between my breasts. "You're perfect, you know that? So fucking perfect—and mine."

I wanted to tell him no one could ever possibly be perfect, but his mouth engulfed my left nipple, sucking it against the roof of his mouth. I lost my entire train of thought, combing my fingers through his hair and holding him against me.

Whatever he was doing with his mouth, it felt so fucking good. I didn't know my nipples were so sensitive, or that he could make me fall apart just by sucking and scraping his teeth over the engorged points. He moved from one nipple to the other, devouring them each in turn until I was mindless and incoherent, needing relief so badly from the pressure building deep between my thighs that I would have sold my soul for just a taste of it.

When he moved farther down my body, I whimpered my protest, but his lips left a damp trail in his wake until he reached my pelvic bone. Dark eyes looked up at me, silently asking me if this was what I wanted.

"Please," I panted, feeling like I might pass out if he didn't kiss me where I ached the most. "I hurt so bad, Braxton. Make it stop."

"Ah, Kitten," he groaned, his breath fanning over my wet folds. "You should have said you were in pain."

"I… Oh God!" I cried out as he brushed his tongue over my pulsing clit and then sucked it between his lips. Stars flashed before my eyes, and I quickly clenched them closed, but they continued to burst behind my lids. I pushed my hips up, grinding against his face in search of fulfillment that was just beyond my reach.

Braxton thrust two fingers inside me, barely going deep enough to press against the barrier that proclaimed me as an innocent. That was all I needed before I was screaming his name. Everything inside me exploded and fused back together in a single instant, shattering and melding into place so rapidly I was sure I lost consciousness for a few seconds before reality set back in.

Gasping for breath, I opened my eyes to find Braxton pushing his basketball shorts down his legs.

Holy hell.

I had no idea how he was going to fit inside me without splitting me in half. He was so thick and long, I was sure he would spear right through me and pierce my heart.

He wrapped his fingers around his shaft, pumping himself up and down as he stood over me, the tip leaking thick, creamy liquid I suddenly had the urge to taste.

"I know you're on the pill, and I'm clean, baby. There's been no one since I lost my leg. But if you aren't comfortable with me going bare—"

"I want to feel you," I interrupted him, and his eyes became hooded.

Braxton climbed over me, supporting himself with one hand while he guided his cock to my entrance. The tip skimmed over my swollen clit, making me jerk in renewed pleasure, a weak moan leaving me as I spread my legs wider in an attempt to accommodate him.

We both gasped when the head of his cock pushed inside me. I felt him begin to shake as he thrust into me until he broke that thin barrier. Remorse filled his eyes when our gazes locked. "I'm sorry, baby," he gritted out before pushing his hips forward and tearing through.

I bit my lip to keep from crying out in pain, but it quickly faded, followed by the most intense feeling of…fullness. I squirmed underneath him, but I couldn't escape the feeling no matter how I shifted.

The entire time, Braxton remained completely still above me, letting me take as long to adjust to his invasion as I needed. I could tell it cost him. His jaw was clenched hard, sweat dripping down his face and chest, his breathing labored.

Lifting my hand, I cupped the side of his face. "It's okay," I assured him. "It doesn't hurt anymore."

"Are you sure? I don't want to cause you pain, Kitten."

I shifted under him again, moaning at the delicious fullness now. "You feel so good, Brax. Please move."

"Baby," he growled. "You feel so fucking good. Nothing has ever been this good."

I felt myself glowing under his words even as my body began to quicken with every thrust of his hips. I'd dreamed of this—one more first with the only man I'd ever wanted to have every first with—and reality was a million times better than any fantasy I'd had over the years.

He rocked his hips against me, his thrusts becoming harder, more demanding. I liked that he was losing control. That he couldn't hold on to that superhero-like willpower of his that he must have been exerting for so damn long.

"Baby," he growled. "I'm gonna come. Want you with me." His thumb grazed over my clit, and suddenly I was hanging right on the edge again.

"Braxton!" I cried, my nails biting into his sides. "Harder, please. I'm almost… I'm going to… Oh fuck!"

His hips stopped as soon as my orgasm hit me, and he just held himself over me, watching as I fell apart for him while he was deep inside me. Panting, I looked up at him through my lashes, barely able to keep my eyes open after two powerful releases.

"Kitten," he growled, his hips suddenly pistoning into me as if he had no control over his own body.

His cock became even harder and more engorged inside me, and with the next thrust, his entire body stiffened. Braxton threw his head back, a look of pure agony on his face as he bellowed, "Goddamn, Kitten," and exploded inside me.

I felt him going off inside me, the liquid proof of his release filling me. It was hot and thick, and it felt so good, my entire body trembled with a mini orgasm.

Exhausted, he fell on top of me, his delicious weight pressing me deeper into the mattress. I stroked my fingers up and down his muscular back while he tried to catch his breath. But only a minute later, he was lifting his head, cursing himself for crushing me.

"Sorry, Kitten," he murmured, turning onto his side and pulling me in close. Our naked bodies were still covered in sweat, and I shivered because the heat wasn't enough to warm me after having his warmth blanket me moments before.

Reaching down, he grabbed the comforter and pulled it up over us. "Are you okay?" he asked quietly, kissing me tenderly. "Did I…hurt you?"

I quickly shook my head. "I loved everything you did to me," I told him honestly, and I felt the tension release from his muscles.

Kissing me again, he tucked my head under his chin and let out a heavy exhale. "Which room do you want to make ours? This one is a little smaller than mine, but I'm okay with whichever one you want to stay in."

I gasped in surprise. "You want us to share a room?"

I felt the vibrations of his deep laugh all the way to the tips of my toes, my nipples hardening instantly. "Kitten, you are mine now. I'm not sleeping anywhere but beside you from here on out."

Everything inside me melted. A content smile lifted my lips, and I closed my eyes, welcoming sleep.

Chapter 14
Nevaeh

I didn't have a Monday class, so I slept in the next morning and then vegged out around the house all day. Having traveled so much my entire life, my body was used to it, so jet lag wasn't something I suffered from. But after the weekend I'd just had, I was slow-moving and just wanted to curl up into a ball on the couch while eating comfort food.

Braxton stayed with me the whole time, and while it didn't make the heartache I felt over my dad go away, it did make it easier to handle. I didn't cry, but when it seemed like I was going to, he would distract me in ways that left me mewling like the kitten he called me.

By the time I left for my first class on Tuesday, I no longer felt like I was going to crumble at every single thought of Daddy and his illness. Like always, Braxton walked me to campus, and we stopped for coffee at the café. In the beginning, Braxton walking me to class had annoyed the hell out of me. It was as if he thought I was a little kid who needed a big, strong man to hold my hand and fight all my battles. But over time, I'd gotten used to it, and if I was honest, I'd grown to like it. Now that we were together, I was all too happy to let him be his normal alpha self and hold my hand while we walked to my classes.

With his hand at the small of my back, we approached the counter. "You want a muffin, baby?" he asked as he gave the guy behind the register our drink orders. Braxton knew my favorite, and I hadn't even had to tell him what I wanted.

"Do they have any double chocolate?" I asked hopefully. I felt like I'd gained a good ten pounds from all the carbs I'd gorged on the day before, but I didn't even care.

"There are two left," the barista told him.

"We'll take both to go," Braxton told him and handed over his card.

I'd given up trying to pay for my own things a long time ago. In the past two years, I'd rarely had to use the cards my parents had given me because no matter what it was or how much it cost, Braxton always paid for my stuff. I'd felt bad about him spending money on me until he told me to just let him take care of me.

When he'd turned eighteen, he'd gotten his trust fund, and while I didn't know how much that was, I knew he never had to work again if he didn't want to. But he still worked for Seller Security, and he and Barrick had big plans for the company when Barrick finally took over from his stepfather. The cousins were going to become business partners, and I had faith the two of them would make a formidable duo in the world of security.

While he was getting our drinks and food, I walked over to an empty table and sat to wait. I didn't check my social media feed often, but I'd ignored it for over five days, so I opened the app to see if there was anything going on with Arella or one of my many cousins. I didn't expect them to keep me constantly up-to-date with what was going on in their lives, so I just let their social media tell me what was happening with them.

I wasn't surprised to see the first picture in my feed was of my sister. It was who she was with that gave me pause. That along with the moon eyes she was giving Jordan Moreitti, who had his arm around her, grinning at the camera as they took a selfie on the beach.

Arella wasn't boy crazy, which I had to give her credit for. Boys were the ones who got crazy over her. As beautiful and talented as she was, I didn't blame them. But Jordan was older than her and, more to the point, a total player. Given that my sister was only sixteen and I knew Moreitti didn't go for jailbait, Arella was only going to break her heart if she thought she had a future with Mia's best friend.

Next in my feed, I saw the twins. I knew which one was Lyric from the way he grinned—it was more easygoing, whereas Luca's was always full of mischief. Luca was sweaty, his hair plastered to his skull and forehead, obviously having just finished football practice.

He was on the defense; that was all I understood of his position on the team, and I really didn't care to learn more about it. But he'd been offered a full ride to some college in Texas and several in the SEC. He hadn't picked which one he was going to attend yet, but no matter what he chose, it was going to cause issues for him.

Lyric, however, wasn't into sports. He was more artistic, and given his obsession with ink lately, I wouldn't be surprised if he became a tattoo artist and opened his own shop one day.

In the background, I saw a group of cheerleaders eyeballing my twin cousins like they were pieces of meat, and I nearly rolled my eyes. It was Lyric's post, and the caption was short: *Feeling cute, might bang the whole cheer squad later. IDK.*

Seeing the reactions below it, I wasn't surprised at the eye-roll emoji my cousin Violet had commented with. Sighing, I kept scrolling until something caught my attention. My eyes scanned over the post, reading everything—twice—before it all clicked in my head.

It wasn't Braxton's post, but because he was tagged in it, I was seeing it in my feed. There was a picture of him in a tux, standing on some grand staircase with an older couple—his parents, from what I'd read. And beside them stood a beautiful blonde in a dress that would have rivaled any celebrity on the red carpet at the Grammys, diamonds dripping down her neck like melting ice.

She had dark blond hair that was pulled to the side in an elegant twist, her makeup expertly applied and showcasing her bone structure. Her brown eyes looked up at Braxton like he hung the moon, and I had to read the post again to make sure I hadn't read it wrong.

Collins and Hamilton wedding scheduled for the post-Christmas season as the two families prepare for their new grandchild.

With the birth of Braxton Collins and Darcy Hamilton's first child, the two dynastical families will become one formidable business empire. Braxton and Darcy are both only children and met in high school. The two have been engaged since their graduation four years ago, but plans were put on hold due to Braxton's injury while serving in the Marines. Belinda Hamilton has hinted that her son's upcoming nuptials will rival any royal wedding in history.

Heart pounding, I skimmed my eyes over the picture again. The ring on Darcy Hamilton's finger was huge and flashy, something that made a statement and screamed for attention. I thought it was ugly and made her fingers look pudgy, but she didn't seem to care as she gazed adoringly at her fiancé. Mr. and Mrs. Collins were beaming proudly at their son and future daughter-in-law.

I stood so quickly, my chair fell back with a loud crash, tears blinding me. Grabbing my backpack, I hurried toward the door.

"Kitten?" Braxton was still standing at the counter, waiting for our drinks.

I shot him a glare through my tears and continued toward the exit. "Baby, what's wrong?"

Shaking my head, I pushed open the door without looking back. I couldn't believe what I'd just read. There was no way Braxton was engaged to someone else. No, he just wouldn't do that. He fucking wouldn't. No way he would ask someone to marry him and then fly across the country to celebrate my birthday with me. Any more than he would cheat by making love to me.

Yet the picture spoke volumes. He looked remarkably like his father, but he had his mother's eyes. And there was that ring and the blonde who couldn't keep the stars out of her eyes. All of it posted by a legitimate news channel.

My heart was breaking. I couldn't suck in a deep enough breath.

It couldn't be true. Braxton wouldn't do that to me. He knew how much I cared about him, how much I loved him, and how long I'd waited for us to be together. He would not break my heart like that.

Would he?

The fact that I even had to question it pissed me off. This on top of getting the news about my dad was too much, damn it. My heart couldn't take any more of this shit.

Strong hands caught me around the waist from behind, stopping me in my tracks. Keeping one hand on my side, Braxton walked in front of me, his face tense as he met my gaze. "What the hell is wrong with you? Why did you storm out like that?"

Lifting my phone, I shoved the picture of him with his parents and fiancée in his face. "What the fuck is this?" I demanded, going on the offensive and watching his face as he looked at the screen.

His jaw clenched as he took my phone from me and groaned. "Fuck. I should have known it would get out like that. My parents don't have social media, though, so I didn't consider it."

"Is it true?" I cringed when I heard the catch in my voice, hating that I didn't sound stronger. My anger was already dying down, and the heartbreak was winning.

He cupped each side of my face in his hands. "No, baby. No. Of course it's not true."

"Then why is this a big story on a reputable news site? This isn't fake news, Brax. It's a legit site."

Muttering a curse, he touched his lips to the corner of my mouth before pulling back so our eyes locked. "Because my parents want it to be true. They're delusional if they actually think I'm going to marry Darcy, though."

"Just who is Darcy to you anyway?"

His lips twisted in a pained grimace. "She was my high school girlfriend. And before you ask, yes, I did ask her to marry me back then. But I regretted it almost as soon as I did."

"You loved her?" He shrugged, and jealousy twisted in my gut. "Do you still?"

"Fuck no!" he exclaimed, his hands dropping to my waist and pulling me closer. "I love *you,* Nevaeh. Listen to me. I don't even think I ever loved Darcy back then. It was more infatuation and the fact that she was good in bed."

My jealousy wasn't getting any better with his explanation. If anything, I only wanted to rip

Darcy's hair out more and more with every word out of his mouth.

"When I lost my leg, she didn't want anything to do with me, and I was relieved to be finished with her without having to break it off myself. I swear to you, there is nothing—absolutely nothing—going on between the two of us."

His vehement denial calmed some of my doubts, but I was still hurt he hadn't told me this had gone on at the party his parents had forced him to attend. Yet I understood why he hadn't. I'd been a mess all weekend, so of course, he wasn't going to unload all of that on me when I was dealing with Daddy's illness.

"No secrets," I told him, forcing myself to relax against him. "Promise me we won't keep anything from each other. No matter how big or small."

"No secrets," he vowed, brushing his lips softly over mine. "I'll tell you everything. Now, let's go get our stuff so I can walk your fine ass to your math class."

"Only if you tell me you love me again," I murmured.

He brushed my hair back from my face, his dark eyes full of need and adoration. "I love you, Kitten. Always."

Chapter 15
Braxton

After leaving Nevaeh at the door to her class, I met Lyla on the edge of campus. She was helping me shop for Christmas because I sucked so royally at it.

She sat in the back of the town car, the driver one of the many guards her brother had hired from Seller's after one of his other men had kidnapped Lyla and her stepdaughter, Josie. Getting in beside her, I tossed her the list of names I needed to buy for and leaned my head back against the seat with a groan.

"Saw the picture of you and that slore Darcy with Aunt Belinda and Uncle Miles," she commented casually. "What kind of acid were those three on over the weekend? I mean, shit, do they actually think they can play with your life like that?"

"They need professional help, that's for fucking sure. They are seriously delusional if they think I'm going to play along and marry that bitch. It's already messing with Nevaeh and me. I hadn't told her what happened at the party yet because of everything going on with her dad, and then she saw the picture in her social media."

I'd nearly lost my mind when I'd seen her run out of the café with tears in her eyes. She'd shot me a glare, and I'd suddenly felt like I was gasping for air. When she'd shoved her phone in my face, I'd wanted to tear my parents and Darcy apart with my bare hands.

"That sucks. But she's cool now, right? You two are okay?"

I nodded. "Yeah, we're good. She knows I wouldn't marry Darcy even if they paid me a billion dollars."

Lyla turned in her seat to face me. "I'm not worried about the wedding thing. It's that she was talking about a baby. I mean, she knows better than to say shit like that if it's not true. Yeah, okay, sure, she could say she had a miscarriage if it really came down to it. But what if she's not making it up?" She frowned, pressing her lips into a hard line. "Maybe she really is pregnant and wants you to play baby daddy to this kid?"

I sat up straight, tension filling every muscle. "Ah fuck, Ly. What if you're right?"

"I suggest you find out one way or the other, little cuz."

"How the hell do I do that?" I asked with a groan. "It's not like she's going to tell me the truth if I point-blank ask her if she's knocked up."

"Well, I doubt any doctor's office would tell you if she was a patient there or not because of HIPAA, so that's out."

"Fuck," I muttered, scrubbing my hands over my face.

"Don't worry. We'll figure this out. I have an idea…" She trailed off, a devious grin lifting at her lips as she picked up her phone lying on the seat between us. "I'm going to need Mia's help, though."

Ten minutes later, we were picking up Mia and driving toward my parents' house instead of the mall. Christmas shopping could wait, but finding out if Darcy was actually pregnant or not wouldn't.

Mia was looking green as usual as she sat on the other side of Lyla. "This baby is really working you over," Lyla murmured sympathetically.

"I'm never getting pregnant again," she said with a moan. "I haven't eaten in days. I'm lucky if I can keep down fluids."

"Well, we will find you the best doctor and get you taken care of, my friend." Lyla patted her on the shoulder as the driver pulled up in front of my parents' mansion.

I didn't particularly like Lyla's idea, but it was the only one we had at the moment, so I had little choice but to follow along. Stepping out of the car, I walked around to help Mia out and kept close to her in case she tripped as we walked up the steps to the front door.

Lyla was already ringing the doorbell, and moments later, the housekeeper pulled the heavy door open with a welcoming smile. My father was at work, but my mother was always at home during the week. The housekeeper led us down to the library, where my mother was sitting with Julia Hamilton. On the table between them were wedding invitation samples and other things that made no sense to me, but they looked like they had to do with wedding preparation.

The housekeeper announced us, then left the room to retrieve refreshments while my mother stood, shock on her face as she crossed the room to greet us. "Darling," she murmured. "What a wonderful surprise."

I barely refrained from rolling my eyes, and I kissed her cheek. "Lyla and Mia couldn't come to the party Friday night, and they wondered if you needed any help planning the wedding."

I had to force myself not to spit the word "wedding" at her, instead giving her a tight smile.

"How wonderful, darling." Turning with a beaming smile, she embraced Lyla then shook Mia's hand. "It's so good to see you again, dear." Her eyes widened when she took in Mia's sickly appearance and the sweat beading her forehead and upper lip. "Are you feeling well?"

Mia swallowed and gave my mother a grim smile. "Morning sickness is the devil," she said with a weak laugh. "It's not contained to just the morning, so I have it all day long."

"Oh goodness," Julia Hamilton exclaimed as she came over to join us. "Darcy had it for weeks until we got her in to see her OB/GYN. Isn't that right, Braxton?"

My eyes widened at her asking me about her daughter's morning sickness. How the fuck would I know when I hadn't even seen her daughter in years up until a few days ago?

But it confirmed one thing.

Darcy was pregnant.

And apparently her mother thought I was the father.

What the actual fuck?

"I just found out that I'm pregnant," Mia told her. "So I haven't found a doctor yet. Would you mind suggesting your daughter's?"

"Not at all." Walking back over to the table, she picked up her phone and came back to us. "Here it is, dear. Tell them Julia Hamilton recommended you, and they will fit you in immediately."

"Auntie Belinda," Lyla said, putting her arm through my mother's. "What can we help you with? I want to make sure Braxton's wedding is perfect, and since he doesn't have any sisters, Mia and I want to step in and help you with all the details."

"That is so kind of you two, darling. Come and look at these beautiful invitations Julia and I are considering…"

For the next hour, the four of them talked about the wedding, and I had to grit my teeth and bite my tongue to keep from yelling at my mother that there wasn't going to be a fucking wedding. Instead, I texted Barrick to ask him to pick up Nevaeh from her class and make sure she got to her next one safely.

By the time the girls made an excuse to leave, I was silently seething.

Darcy really was pregnant and using this wedding to push her unborn baby off on me. Did she really think she could get away with that and I would just fall in line with her plans?

Fuck that shit.

"We need to find out who the father is," Lyla said as we rode back to the house. "I think we should put a tail on her."

"Whatever. Just do it. I want to know everything she does ASAP before I confront her."

Mia leaned forward to look at me over my cousin. "What do we tell Nevaeh?"

"Fuck," I groaned, remembering my promise not to keep anything from her. But I doubted she would be happy to go along with Lyla's plan for me to play excited groom for my mother and Julia Hamilton until I figured out the rest of Darcy's game. With finals only a week away and her dad's illness and upcoming surgery, I didn't want to add more stress to her already heavy load. "Mia, what do I do?"

Her brow scrunched up for a moment before she blew out a frustrated sigh. "I don't think we should tell her about any of this yet. She seems so fragile right now. I hate keeping her in the dark about anything, but after seeing how she was on the flight home and then yesterday…"

"Yeah," I muttered, my gut twisting in dread. "After next week, we will be back in California until the holidays are over. I can tell her everything once she's done with finals and has had time to chill for a few days."

Both Mia and Lyla agreed it was the best plan for the moment, but even though it was mine, I wasn't sure if it was actually the right thing to do. If Nevaeh found out I was keeping this from her, she was going to be pissed—and maybe hurt. Which I couldn't fucking stand. No matter what kind of pain my kitten experienced, it drove me crazy. And if I was the one to cause that pain…

It would kill me.

Chapter 16
Nevaeh

Mom taught me to cook from a young age. She loved it when my sisters and brother and I helped her in the kitchen. Of everyone in our extended family, I liked to think my parents and siblings were the closest unit. When I was a kid, they would take me everywhere with them, and even though Daddy had a crazy-busy schedule and they could have easily afforded a dozen nannies, they never used one.

Cooking was one of my favorite things to do, especially when I was missing Mom. Mia and the guys loved that I could and would cook for them. Otherwise, it was breakfast foods or takeout for every meal.

Pulling out the freshly baked cookies from the oven was like starting a stampede. I heard Braxton's and Barrick's feet stomping as they sprinted into the kitchen and grabbed themselves one before I'd even placed the tray of cookies on top of the stove.

"Fuck, if I didn't love Mia so much, I would marry you, Nevaeh," Barrick told me around his huge bite of scalding-hot cookie.

I laughed, because that was what he said every time I baked something decadent. Transferring the rest of the cookies to the cooling rack, I turned to find Braxton leaning against the sink beside the refrigerator. He was eating his cookie a lot slower than his cousin, which made me stop and take better notice of him.

By this point, he should have been working on his second or third cookie, despite their being so hot he would burn his tongue on the melted chocolate chips. He didn't care, though, because he would wash them down with ice-cold milk and keep eating until either the cookies ran out or I took them away from him. Instead, he just stood there, barely nibbling on the first cookie that was rapidly cooking in his hand, a deep frown between his brows, almost as if he were in pain.

Concerned, I crossed to him and touched his forehead. "Are you feeling okay?" He didn't feel hot, and his skin wasn't pale. Yet I got the feeling something was seriously off with him.

He caught my hand and pulled it down so he could press my palm to the center of his chest. "I love you."

Everything inside me melted. Stepping closer to him, I wrapped my free arm around his waist. Since the first "I love you," he'd been saying it often, and every single time felt just as good as that first one. I was never going to get tired of him saying those three words. "I love you back," I told him. "But that doesn't explain why you are barely eating your favorite cookie."

"Kitten, you're my favorite cookie, and I would rather eat you than anything else." With a heated, wicked gleam in his eyes, he stuffed the rest of his cookie into his mouth and swept me up into his arms. I barely had time to realize Barrick had left the kitchen before Braxton was carrying me to my room.

Our room, now that Braxton had moved his things in there. Sasha lifted her head off the bed when we walked in. "Sasha, out," he commanded gently, and she slowly climbed off our bed and trotted out of the room.

Shutting the door with his foot, he carried me to the bed and set me down carefully. It was as if he thought I might break, and that made me smile even as he was lowering his head to devour my mouth.

"Love you so fucking much, Kitten," he said with a groan as he started pulling off my clothes. "Never going to let you go."

"Good." That single word turned into a moan when he pushed my legs apart roughly and lowered his head. His lips latched on to my clit, and for a long, long while, he didn't treat me like I was fragile at all.

Hours later, I lifted my head from his chest. He didn't look like he was in pain any longer, but there was a pensiveness to him that told me he wasn't completely with me in the postcoital blissfulness I was currently enjoying while he rubbed his callused fingers up and down my naked back.

"Is something wrong?" I asked, worried about him. Braxton didn't go dark often, but when he did, he drew into himself. I hated the distance I felt him putting between himself and everyone else.

"Hmm?" Blinking a few times, he finally focused his eyes on me, and whatever he was thinking was shoved into a box, locked away from me. I didn't want anything between us, but I would let him keep those deep thoughts to himself until he was ready to talk to me about it. I knew he didn't like to talk about the accident that had cost him his leg, and I wouldn't force him to relive it if he didn't want to.

"Fuck," he muttered, pushing my hair back from my face. "You are so beautiful, Nevaeh. Inside and out. Waiting for you was the hardest thing I've ever had to do but worth every second now that I get to hold you like this."

"The hardest? Really? Even more so than your accident?"

He nodded. "Losing my leg was bad, baby. But the last two years, sitting beside you without getting to touch you the way I wanted, seeing your smiling face without being able to kiss these perfect lips, that was the worst kind of torture. In my heart, we have been together from the moment I saw you. We just had to wait before telling the world."

Smiling happily, I dropped my head back onto his chest. "You keep calling me perfect, but I'm not. No one is."

"You are," he argued stubbornly. "And you'll never convince me otherwise."

Laughing, I snuggled against him more, wanting to burrow into him completely so that we were always connected. "Okay, I'm not going to try to change your mind anymore. I like that I'm perfect in your eyes."

We stayed like that for several more minutes until I heard his stomach growl. Looking up at him, I grinned. "You're probably all out of luck with the cookies. We left them unsupervised hours ago. Barrick no doubt finished them off long before Mia even had to go to work." I stood up unashamedly, loving the way his breath hitched when he watched me walk to the closet to find something to wear. "Do you want me to make dinner or go out for something?"

"All I want is standing right in front of me," he said, and I glanced at him over my shoulder. His dark eyes were on my ass, and I gave it a little shake, causing him to groan like he was in pure agony. "Kitten, come back to bed."

Laughing happily, I pulled on a bra and then one of his shirts that was hanging beside mine. "No way. I'm starving. But after we eat, you can have all the dessert you want," I promised with a wink.

"Compromise," he said, sitting up. "I order pizza and whatever else you want. And you come back to bed until it gets here. Then, we eat in bed, and after, I get to enjoy as much of my dessert as I want all night long."

My body turned hot with renewed desire at his suggestion. Glancing down at the T-shirt I'd pulled on, I shrugged and pulled it back over my head. Tossing the bra on the floor of the closet, I walked back to him and crawled up the end of the bed toward him.

His hungry gaze devoured me as I took my time until I was straddling his hips. "You drive a hard bargain, Mr. Collins. One I simply cannot refuse."

Chapter 17
Nevaeh

I walked out of my last final of the semester with a throbbing headache and an intense need for coffee and something decadent. Tests were normally nothing for me, but with all that was going on with Daddy, it took everything I had to focus on the exams.

My fingers felt chilled when I touched them to my temples as I stepped out into the snowy late afternoon. Braxton wasn't waiting on me since he had his own finals to finish, so I headed straight for the campus café without glancing around for him. As I walked, I turned on my phone and thought about everything I still needed to pack for the trip home the following day.

PopPop was supposed to meet me at the airport since Mia wasn't flying home until closer to Christmas. Luckily, she'd gotten an appointment with a reputable local OB/GYN the week before, and after a few days of following his advice, her morning sickness was starting to become manageable. I'd been worried about her, because for a few days, she hadn't even been able to keep down liquids for long. Barrick took her to the emergency room at one point the day before she saw her doctor just for IV fluids.

After stopping at the café for a large cup of my favorite coffee, I walked home. It felt strange being without Braxton, lonely. I missed him even though I'd just seen him a little over two hours before, and I knew I would see him again by dinner. Thankfully, he was going to fly with me to California the next day, but he would be at Mia's parents' house instead of mine.

Mom knew I was with Braxton now, but neither of us had mentioned it to Daddy yet. I didn't want to know his reaction to our new relationship, and I figured he would freak the hell out if I asked him if my boyfriend could stay with us—or actually sleep in my room.

By the time I got to the house, I already had my keys out. I was freezing despite the thick winter coat I was wearing and the hot coffee I was still sipping. Putting the key in the lock, I started to open the door when a car I didn't recognize pulled up in the driveway.

Frowning, I watched as a blonde got out of the driver's side. Her eyes skimmed dispassionately over the house before landing on me. Dressed in a black designer jumpsuit that showcased her willowy body and an open wool trench coat, she walked with grace in her gold heels despite the ice that was forming on the concrete walkway. I knew exactly who she was from the picture of Braxton and his parents taken the week before.

Darcy Hamilton.

Something darkened in her eyes as she came up the walkway toward me. "Hi, is Brax home, by any chance? I was supposed to meet him for coffee earlier, but he was a no-show."

Pushing the door open, I dropped my backpack inside the house and turned to face her. "No, he's taking his Communications final. Would you like me to give him a message?"

She stopped only a few feet from me, thrusting her hands into her coat and glancing over my shoulder like she expected Braxton to pop up behind me at any moment. "Yeah, you can tell him to call me. We have a lot to sort out before the wedding next month."

"You're delusional," I told her, my anger spiking rapidly. "There is no way in hell he is going to marry you. He's with me." My phone started ringing, and I pulled it out of my pocket. Seeing it was my mom, I answered it. "Hey, Mom—"

"Did you finish your final?" she asked, her voice sounding strained.

"Yes. About thirty minutes ago." Darcy shifted, distracting me. "You should leave," I told her, pulling my mouth away from the phone. "Before I call the cops. Although having your crazy ass committed sounds appealing as hell right now."

"Nevaeh, I need to tell you something," Mom was saying in my ear while Darcy pulled an elegant envelope out of her pocket and thrust it toward me.

"Here, since you don't believe me about the wedding, take a look for yourself." She pushed it against my chest when I just glared down at it.

"Nevi, honey, something happened this morning. Daddy…" I suddenly realized Mom's voice was full of tears even as my fingers folded around the envelope.

Feeling as if I was having a weird out-of-body experience, I listened to Mom telling me that Daddy was in the hospital and that his surgery was being moved up. That as soon as they got him and Uncle Shane prepped, they would be doing the transplant.

While I heard it all, I felt the tears start to flow because I wasn't there to tell Daddy I loved him before he went into surgery. I opened the envelope with fingers that trembled and pulled out a wedding invitation.

"Braxton and his cousin Lyla picked out that invitation with my mother and his last week. I think Mother even said his cousin's pregnant fiancée was with them and agreed this was the perfect invitation for our wedding." She smiled coldly, making me want to scratch up her pretty face. "You can keep that, sweetie. Brax and I would just love it if you could make it." She turned to walk back to her car but paused at the end of the walkway. "And no worries about you being with him. I don't mind sharing him. All guys have a mistress these days, right?"

Lifting her hand, she gave me a small wave and, still laughing, walked to her car.

"Nevaeh, sweetheart." Mom's voice penetrated my mind as Darcy pulled out of the driveway. Her voice was so full of emotion, I doubted she'd heard or even realized I'd had company. "Aunt Emmie has sent a car for you, and it will be there soon. Don't worry about packing anything. Mia will bring your things when she comes. Just grab your ID. You're on the first flight home, and it leaves in less than an hour. Someone from security will meet you at the entrance to the airport and escort you to the gate so you don't have to worry about missing your plane."

Closing my eyes, I sucked in a deep breath and tried to pull myself together mentally. There would be plenty of time later to digest what Darcy had just told me. For now, I had to get to the airport and home. I didn't remember half of what Mom said, so I didn't know why Daddy was having emergency surgery, but I did know my family needed me a hell of a lot more than Braxton did.

"Baby, please say something. You're starting to scare me," Mom cried.

"Tell Daddy I love him," I choked out, each word feeling like it was being torn from my throat. "Give him a kiss for me. Tell him…"

What? Not to die?

Tears poured from my eyes at that horrible thought, and I choked back a sob. "Tell Uncle Shane I love him too."

"I will, honey. And you know they both love you. Just be strong, my baby. Everything will be okay."

"Don't make promises you can't keep, Mom," I told her and hung up before I completely broke down. She didn't need to hear me sobbing like a shattered little girl when she already had so many other things to worry about.

Crumpling the wedding invitation in my fist, I reached back into the house for my backpack. It had my wallet in it, and apparently, that was all I needed. As I shut and locked the front door again, a black sedan pulled up at the end of the driveway. A man in a suit stepped out, sympathy on his face when he saw my tears.

"Miss Nevaeh Stevenson?" I nodded numbly as I quickly walked toward him, and he opened the back door for me. "I'll get you to the airport, Miss Stevenson. Don't you worry about a thing."

Nodding mutely, I climbed into the back seat and shoved the wedding invitation into the backpack with my books. Scrubbing a hand over my damp cheeks, I texted Mom that I was on my way to the airport and I would see her as soon as I could.

Chapter 18
Braxton

As soon as the plane touched down and they let everyone disembark, I was running. It hurt like fucking hell because I didn't have my running blade on, but I didn't care about the physical pain.

All I could think about was that my kitten had had to make the flight to California all on her own while worrying about her dad. She must have been scared out of her mind, and I wasn't there to hold her, to tell her it was all going to be okay. She was so upset about everything going on that she hadn't even texted or called me.

I'd gotten out of my final earlier and turned on my phone, to find Mia had blown up my messages, telling me what was going on.

Drake Stevenson had woken up in agony and vomiting uncontrollably. Lana rushed him to the hospital, where the doctors said they needed to do the surgery immediately, not to wait for the date they had originally planned. Nevaeh's Uncle Shane was told to go straight to the hospital so they could prep him. Thankfully, it was so early he hadn't had breakfast or even coffee yet. Otherwise, they would have had to wait. The surgery would take anywhere from four to eight hours, depending on complications, and by the time I'd gotten Mia's messages, both men had already been in the operating room for over an hour.

Once I knew what was going on and that Nevaeh was already on her way, nothing could have stopped me from getting to California. Luckily for me, Mia's mom was some kind of miracle worker who predicted everything, and she already had a car service waiting for me just off campus to take me to the airport. A ticket had been sent to my phone, and I was escorted straight to my gate when I got there. I had an hour wait, but at least there were no connections for my flight, so I got there as quickly as possible with no delays.

Running out of the airport, I saw a driver holding up a sign with my name on it, and I sprinted toward him. The man had the back door of the town car already open by the time I got to him, and I jumped in, telling him to move his ass.

As I wiped sweat off my brow, I pulled out my phone and tried to call Nevaeh again. Her phone had been off earlier, so I'd left a message telling her I loved her and would be there as soon as I could.

Now, her phone rang and rang, but she didn't answer. Figuring she was with her mom and the rest of her family and not paying attention to her phone, I sat back and closed my eyes. My leg was already throbbing, but I blocked out that pain, hoping both Drake and Shane made it through this.

Traffic was total hell, and it felt like it took hours to get to the hospital. I texted Emmie when the driver said we were only ten minutes away, and there was someone waiting for me when he pulled up at the back entrance. There had been flashing cameras and news vans in the front parking lot when the driver passed it. It was one of Seller's men and Harris Cutter, who greeted me with a handshake when I stepped out of the car.

"How are they?" I asked as we hurried inside before any stray vulturous paps pounced on us.

"We got news when they took part of Shane's liver that he came through it easily. He's still in recovery right now, though, and they will only let Harper back to see him, but everything seems to be good on his end. We haven't had any news about Drake yet, though." He pushed the elevator button, and it opened immediately.

"And Nevaeh? How is she holding up?"

He pressed his lips together for a moment before he blew out a heavy sigh. "I'll have to let you determine that for yourself, man. She seems…off."

Off? I didn't know what the fuck that meant, but I kept my mouth shut as we rode up. When the elevator opened a few moments later, there were four more of Seller's men standing at attention. One moved forward, asking for my ID.

Knowing the drill, I produced it and got a chin lift in acknowledgment when he realized who I was. One day, I was going to be this guy's boss, but that day wasn't this one.

Harris led me down a short corridor to a waiting room where two more security men were standing. Inside, the room was almost full to capacity yet eerily quiet, almost as if everyone was afraid to speak.

I scanned the room until I found Nevaeh. She was sitting with all three of her sisters, her little brother sitting on her lap. The two youngest sisters each had their heads on Nevaeh's shoulders, while

Arella clutched at one of her hands. None of them were crying, although there was proof they had done plenty of that from their swollen, red eyes and tear tracks down their cheeks.

I moved toward them. As I approached, the younger four all lifted their heads, giving me grim smiles, but Nevaeh didn't move so much as an eyelash. Her gaze was trained straight ahead, her face completely devoid of…everything. There was no emotion, no signs of life in her eyes. If she hadn't been breathing, I would have thought she was a beautiful mannequin.

"Braxton," Lana stopped me before I could reach my kitten, with a chilled hand to my arm.

Seeing the tears that still filled her eyes and the lack of color in her face, I hugged her.

"I'm so glad you're here," she whispered when I pulled back. "Something is wrong with Nevaeh. All she's done since she got here is sit there. Like she is now. She hasn't moved. She hasn't spoken, not one word. I don't know if it's shock or what, but this isn't good for her. I can't get her to drink anything or to eat."

I glanced over Lana's head. Nevaeh's sisters were all whispering something to her, but she didn't seem to hear them.

"Take her for a walk. She needs to cry or scream or hit something." Lana grimaced. "She just needs to come back to us because I can't breathe right now, thinking I might lose her on top of everything else…"

Hearing the hitch in her voice cracked my heart open, and I gave her another hug, promising I would take care of her daughter.

Crouching down in front of the five siblings, I gave Damien a tight smile. "Hey, little dude." I bumped fists with the eight-year-old. "Maybe you can sit on Arella's lap for a little while so I can take your sister for a walk?"

He nodded and jumped down. The movement didn't even budge Nevaeh. She still sat there, staring at nothing, her eyes unblinking behind her glasses. Heavenleigh and Bliss shook their heads at me.

"It's like she's a statue," Bliss murmured quietly. "She's seriously starting to freak me out."

I took both of Nevaeh's hands in mine. Feeling how cold her fingers were, I started rubbing them. "Hey there, Kitten."

She jerked at my special name for her. Her head moved, and she finally blinked, focusing on her surroundings. Shifting her gaze from left to right, she took in the room and all her relatives. Then she looked down at me, and heat filled those blue-gray depths.

"No," she bit out between clenched teeth, and my heart dropped into my stomach. "I don't want you here."

It was my turn to jerk, her words like a physical blow directly to my solar plexus. When she tried to pull her hands from mine, I tightened my hold. "Kitten—"

"I said no!" she screamed and jumped to her feet, forcing her hands from mine. "Get the hell out of here. I don't want to see your lying face. Not now, not ever."

Everyone in the room seemed to move in around us, but they didn't intervene. I stood, trying to reach for her, but she slapped my hands away as two huge tears fell from her eyes. Seeing her tears, I felt my own eyes begin to sting. "Baby, I'm so sorry you had to fly here on your own. If I'd known what was going on, I would have been with you, I swear."

"I'm glad you weren't with me," she spat, pure venom in her words. "Why would I want a cheater like you anywhere near me?"

"What are you talking about?" I demanded, reaching for her again. "You're out of it, Nev. Baby, you're just in shock. Come here. Let me hold you."

"Stay the hell away from me," she raged. "Don't touch me. Don't even speak to me. Ever."

She shoved me, and I was so surprised, I actually took a step back just as she moved away from me and ran toward the door. But before she could open it, a man in sweat-soaked scrubs and a surgical cap walked in. She stopped when he glanced around the room. Her eyes were huge and full of fear when she looked at him, as if she thought he was the grim reaper or something.

"Mrs. Stevenson?" the doctor called out, and Lana practically sprinted to him.

He took her hands in both of his and gave her a reassuring smile. "Everything went beautifully. I couldn't have asked for a better surgery. He came through it with no complications. And as long as he remains stable, you can see him in about an hour."

Everyone in the room collectively released their held breaths. I saw Nevaeh begin to sway, and

I rushed toward her, my arms going around her as her eyes completely lost focus and she fell against me, unconscious. I lifted her into my arms easily.

Lana and Emmie appeared on either side of me while the doctor checked the pulse at her wrist. "She's okay," he said after a tense moment. "I think the relief of getting good news just messed with her blood pressure a bit."

Even as he spoke, Nevaeh moaned in my arms. I kissed her brow, and she opened her eyes. For a fraction of a second, she frowned. "What happened?" she whispered.

"Honey, you passed out." Lana tenderly brushed her daughter's hair back from her face. "But we got good news. Daddy is going to be okay."

Her face lit up, then crumpled when she looked at me. "Let go of me," she seethed.

"Not happening," I told her calmly.

"Wanna bet?" She lifted her head and looked for someone over my shoulder. "Luca. Lyric. Make him put me down."

The two identical beast-like eighteen-year-olds stood without question and marched toward me. I only tightened my hold on Nevaeh. I didn't want to fight anyone during this emotional family moment, but I would kick both their asses if they tried to take her from me.

"Whoa there, killers," Emmie said, cutting off the twins before they could get to me. I wasn't surprised they stopped in their tracks. I was pretty sure she could have told a charging bull to stop and it would listen to her. "Back to your seats," she commanded. "And, Luca? Try to get Violet to drink something. She hasn't had anything since Harper went to sit with Shane."

He nodded as the two of them both returned to their seats. Picking up Violet's hand, he murmured something to her, and she gave a weak nod. He passed her a bottle of water, which she put to her lips and took a small sip.

Emmie turned her focus on Nevaeh next. "Sweetheart, you have been like a zombie from the moment you got here. We all understand that, but you aren't making any sense right now. If something is wrong, you have to tell me so I can make it all better. Okay?"

"What's there not to make sense of?" she demanded, her beautiful face a mask of anger and hurt, making it impossible for me to draw a deep enough breath. When she hurt, I hurt. I wanted to make it all go away, but she was pissed as hell at me. "Braxton's fiancée showed up at the house with their wedding invitation. An invitation your daughter helped him pick out."

Ah fuck.

I didn't know how or when she'd found out about the invitation, but I knew I needed to start explaining. If she would listen. My promise not to keep anything from her was broken, but I had to get her to hear me out.

"Kitten," I began. "It's not what you think. I'm not marrying her."

She snorted and struggled in my arms, but I held on to her easily, refusing to let her go, terrified if she did get out of my arms somehow, I would never get her back into them. "Maybe you should tell that to Darcy, then."

"He isn't," Emmie tried to tell her. "I've been helping him sort out the publicity side of everything for the past few weeks. I promise you, Nevaeh, he is not marrying Darcy Hamilton."

The fight suddenly drained out of her, and that scared me more than when she was struggling to get away. She was giving up, blocking me out. I could practically feel the walls slamming down between us, blocking me from her and her heart. "Whatever. I don't even care right now. I just want to be away from him."

Chapter 19
Nevaeh

The numbness I'd felt since getting on the plane earlier was gone now. I wanted it back. All the emotions that were running riot through me were causing the mother of all headaches, and I wanted to turn them off.

I wanted to feel nothing, think nothing…*be* nothing.

It was too much. Daddy's emergency surgery and finding out my boyfriend planned on marrying someone else, that he'd even picked out their damn wedding invitations, broke something in me. I lost Braxton, and then there was the very large possibility that I could lose my dad…and it hurt so damn badly that I couldn't think. The moment Darcy handed me that wedding invitation, part of me shattered.

I blocked out everything. My senses shut off, and for a while, I couldn't hear, see, feel, taste, or even smell anything. I was just floating somewhere in my head. It was dark there, but quiet and oddly peaceful. There was no lying, cheating boyfriend. My dad wasn't sick or possibly dying. Nothing could touch or hurt me.

Then I heard it.

Kitten.

So tenderly spoken, with love and kindness. The complete opposite of the man he'd been hiding from me—along with his fiancée and all the other lies he'd fed me. How could I have been so wrong about him? How could I have been so stupid as to trust him?

Whatever spell I'd cast over myself broke, and it all came flooding back with a vengeance.

Feeling someone shift beside me, I slowly turned my head. It was only Arella readjusting Damien on her lap. He was eight and already getting tall, but we all babied him and he didn't mind letting us. On the other side of Arella sat Jordan Moreitti, and I honestly didn't know when he'd arrived. I didn't know when anyone had shown up or if they had been there already when I'd gotten there. I didn't remember anything after taking my seat on the plane earlier.

On my other side, sat Bliss and Heavenleigh. I was thankful they surrounded me. That meant Braxton couldn't get close.

He hadn't left. I could feel his eyes on me, and despite refusing to look his way, I knew exactly where he was in the room. He was sitting in a chair in a corner, Mia's brother Jagger beside him. That was where he'd been since Aunt Emmie had told him to put me down. Something he hadn't done right away. It took her using her fire-breather voice before he carried me to the chair I was in presently and then took his current seat on the opposite side of the room from me.

That had been over an hour ago. Mom had been escorted back to see Daddy just a few minutes before, promising us all that she would tell him we loved him. I understood why only one person was allowed back to see him for now, but I wanted to go with her. Needed to see with my own eyes that the doctor hadn't been lying. That he was really okay. Breathing.

Someone crouched down in front of me, and it took me a moment before my eyes finally focused on Lyric. Grasping one of my chilled hands in his much bigger one, he pressed a cup of something hot into it then guided my other hand up so I was holding it with both. "It's hot chocolate. It's all I could find in the cafeteria that I figured you would drink. There isn't a coffee shop in the building, and Aunt Emmie has declared martial law, so we're kind of trapped and can't go across the street to Starbucks."

"Thanks," I told him weakly and lifted the cup to my lips. It tasted slightly bitter yet overly sweet, but the heat dethawed my insides a little, making me shiver. "Why is it so sweet?"

"I added a few extra packets of sweetener," he said sheepishly. "Figured you needed a sugar rush."

"Um, yeah. Thanks." I took another sip, grimacing at how sweet it was, then shrugged and tossed back the rest of the contents. It was hot as hell and burned my mouth, but I welcomed the pain.

Lyric's mouth fell open when I handed him the empty cup. "Are you okay?"

"That's debatable," I told him honestly. "But I'll live."

Leaning forward, he lowered his voice. "Give me the word, and Luca and I will fuck him over, Nevi."

Knowing he and his twin would burn the whole place down if I asked, I shook my head. "No. It's not worth it. But thanks anyway."

"Mia and Barrick are downstairs," I heard Jordan saying to Arella.

Stiffening, I stood. "I need the bathroom," I told Lyric. "Where is it?"

"I'll show you," he offered. He put his arm over my shoulders, guiding me out of the room and down the hall to the bathrooms.

I forced myself to take my time, needing to be away from Braxton's pleading eyes—and yes, hiding from Mia for a little while. I couldn't believe she would betray me like she did, yet for some reason, I didn't doubt what Darcy said about Mia helping Braxton and Lyla pick out the wedding invitations with his mom.

I stayed in the bathroom so long, Lyric opened the door enough so he could ask if I was okay. Grimacing, I washed my hands and walked out, knowing he wouldn't let me hide in there any longer.

But when I stepped out of the bathroom, Braxton was standing there with Lyric, Barrick and Mia right beside him.

I glared at my cousin when she started to step forward to hug me. "Don't even talk to me, Mia. I'm not in the mood to hear your excuses."

She gasped as if I'd hurt her, but I couldn't have cared less. She'd broken my heart just as easily as Braxton had. I thought we were close, family. And if nothing else, I knew family was always supposed to have your back. I didn't want to see her or even hear her voice.

"Nevaeh," she pleaded. "I didn't tell you because of your dad. You've been so upset that I was afraid—"

"Yeah. Great excuse. Use Daddy's illness to hide the fact that you were helping my boyfriend plan his fucking wedding." My laugh was cold, without an ounce of humor. "Thanks for that. Good to know where your loyalties lie." Walking around them, I headed for the waiting room.

"Nev, I'm so sorry," she called after me, tears thickening her voice.

I jerked around to face her. "Take your apology and go fuck yourself, Mia. You and me? We are no longer family. From here on out, stay the hell away from me."

"Nev—" she sobbed, holding out her hands toward me.

I stepped back. "You cry so prettily, Mia. But your tears don't affect me. I'm done with you." I looked at Braxton. His jaw was clenched hard, his face tense and pale. In that moment, I loved and hated him. But I hated myself more. I'd let him break my heart. I'd given him that power over me. And when he gave me that bullshit explanation about the picture of him, Darcy, and his parents, I'd believed him without question. Really, I had no one else to blame but myself. "Both of you."

Lyric stepped between us, his hands raised like a referee calling for a time-out. "Okay, let's all just calm down for a second here. You two are hard to keep up with at times. So, Mia helped Braxton here pick out his wedding invitations? But Braxton is Nevaeh's boyfriend?"

"Don't act cute, Lyric," Mia snapped at him. "Yes, to both. We had to find out if Darcy was actually pregnant or not…"

I felt all the blood drain from my face at the same time Mia trailed off and then pressed her lips together. Barrick muttered something to her I didn't hear, but I was more focused on his cousin.

"You're going to be a father?" I choked out, turning eyes that burned to Braxton.

"No!" He lifted his hands pleadingly as he took a step toward me, but I quickly backed up, putting more distance between us. "Kitten, I swear to you, I'm not the father."

Shaking my head, I kept walking backward, my tears blinding me. "I don't believe you. How could you keep any of this from me? I thought you loved me."

"I do," he rasped. "Baby, I love you more than anyone. You are my other half, the fucking reason I even get out of bed in the mornings. Please, just listen to me. I can explain everything if you will give me five minutes."

"Why?" I cried. "So you can lie to me more? Feed me more bullshit? You promised no secrets, that we would tell each other everything, and yet you kept something as major as this from me. You lied."

"Kitten, you were so distraught over your dad, I didn't want to add more stress on you. I was never going to marry Darcy. It was just an idea Lyla came up with to find out if Darcy was pregnant like she was telling everyone." I made a distressed sound, causing Lyric to move closer to me protectively.

"She is, but it's not mine. I swear on everything I love and hold dear, I'm not the father of her child. Fuck, baby, I hadn't even seen her in years until the night of my parents' party."

"Then who the hell is the father?" I demanded, unsure if I believed him or not.

"I don't know yet. I've had a tail on her for the past week to see what he can find out about her." He moved closer, but I grabbed Lyric's arm and used him as a human shield to keep Braxton away. I could barely see him over my cousin's shoulder, but I was sure everyone in the hospital heard his feral growl, and for a moment, I actually worried about Lyric's safety. "Goddamn it, Nevaeh, let me touch you. I can't stand this distance between us. I'm not marrying Darcy. I'm not the father of her baby. You are the only woman I love, and right now, you are ripping my fucking heart out."

The pain in his voice only made what I was feeling that much more intense, but I refused to give in.

"Having Darcy show up at our door, finding out you were keeping shit from me, that tore my heart out, Braxton!" I yelled at him over Lyric.

"Hey, hey, hey!" I stiffened at the sound of Mom's voice and clutched even tighter at my shield. "Why are you screaming out here?"

I turned to face her. When I saw her ashen face and the tears on her cheeks, my knees went weak. "How is he?" I asked, my breath coming out in gasps.

Her eyes went to everyone before they landed on me, and something softened in her tense face. "He's in pain but good. He told me to tell you how much he loves you." Then she looked at everyone else again. "Mia, I think you should take your friends back to your house. This isn't the time for whatever is going on with you guys, and I won't have Nevaeh more upset than she already is. That is only going to stress Drake out more."

"I agree," Uncle Nik announced, coming out of the men's room. The look on his face told me he must have heard everything. There was something dark in his expression as he looked at his daughter. "After the hell you've put me through for keeping everything from you two years ago, I'm surprised you would keep secrets from anyone, Mia. Least of all from Nevaeh."

"This isn't like that at all," she told him with a stubborn lift of her chin. "I just wanted to protect Nevaeh."

"Yeah, and that was what I was doing with you, but that whole situation ruined our entire relationship, didn't it?" He walked around Braxton and Lyric and put his arm around my shoulders. "Now, whatever you have to say to each other can and will wait until later, Mia. For now, take your ass home and stay there."

Chapter 20
Nevaeh

No one but Mom was allowed to see Daddy for the rest of the night. The doctor wanted him to rest, and depending on his pain level the next day, we would get to see him then.

Mom and Aunt Harper both decided to stay, but they wanted us kids to go home and get some rest. Luca took Violet and Mason home, and one of Aunt Emmie's security team drove me home with Bliss, Heavenleigh, and Damien. But it was Jordan who drove Arella home. I didn't even want to know what was going on there. She was too young, and he was nothing but a player. My sister was going to get her heart broken by him, but I didn't have the energy to argue with her over it.

At home, I made a snack for everyone and then went to take a shower. I felt drained, but when I lay down a short while later, I couldn't get my brain to turn off, so I just stared sightlessly at my ceiling in my darkened bedroom. The house felt too quiet, empty without Mom and Daddy there.

My phone went off, and I reached out blindly to grab it off the side table. Lifting it, I saw it was a text from Braxton and debated the pros and cons of throwing my phone against the wall. But in the end, I just dropped the damn thing back onto the nightstand because it was my only method of immediate contact with Mom. If something happened to Daddy in the middle of the night and she couldn't reach me…

I heard the door open, and I lifted my head off my pillow to find four shadows sneaking in. "Come on," I told them and pulled back my comforter. Patting the bed beside me, I waited until all four of my siblings climbed in before covering us all up.

Damien was the one snuggled up against me, with my three sisters squished up behind him. It was only a queen bed, not made for five people, least of all my squirmy as hell siblings. The mattress protested when Bliss and Heavenleigh twisted and turned until they found a comfortable position.

Despite feeling like hell, I found myself smiling and kissed my baby brother's brow.

"Daddy's really going to be okay…right, Nevi?" I wasn't surprised by the question, but that it was Arella asking it made my heart ache. She was always so confident, so strong like Mom, that I sometimes forgot she could be just as vulnerable as me.

Reaching across the other three, I caught her hand and linked our fingers together. "Yeah, he's going to be fine," I told her. The truth was I didn't know, but my heart wouldn't let me tell her anything but what she—what we all—really needed to hear.

"PopPop said Dad loves Mom so much, there was no way he'd die," Damien said, then yawned loudly. "PopPop said Dad would just make a deal with the man on the other side to come back, and if that didn't work, he'd fight his way back to Mom. Because nothing can keep them apart. Not even death."

"Sounds like something Daddy would do," Heavenleigh said with a choked laugh.

"I want that," Arella said wistfully in the dark.

"What?" Bliss asked, sounding confused.

"Someone who loves me so much, he'd fight anything to hold on to me. Even death or God or whatever else stands in his way." She sighed heavily, and I heard her shifting. "I want someone to love me like Daddy loves Mom. Endlessly. Deathlessly."

"Me too," I whispered.

I'd thought for an all too brief time I'd found someone who loved me just like that. Someone who would put me above everything and everyone else. Who might spend his life cherishing me and our love. Someone who actually needed me.

But then he showed me differently.

A stray tear leaked from the corner of my eye, and I quickly scrubbed it away. I'd thought I was all cried out, but two more tears fell over my lashes. My heart ached, wanting something I knew I would probably never get.

Beside me, Damien began to snore, making my sisters and me laugh quietly. He could sleep anywhere, during anything, and for that, I was kind of jealous of the little brat.

One by one, the others followed Damien into slumber until it was just me awake. Feeling restless, I carefully untangled myself from my brother and tiptoed to the door. Downstairs, I made a pot of coffee and then opened the fridge. It was stocked full of groceries, and I started taking out the fresh herbs and vegetables I would need for homemade chicken noodle soup.

I wasn't sure what Daddy's diet would consist of the next few days, but I did know he loved the soup Mom made. She'd taught my sisters and me how to make it when we were little. I would make a big pot of it and then take some to the hospital later for both Daddy and Uncle Shane.

After putting a pot full of a whole chicken with garlic and herbs on the stove to start to simmer, I began chopping carrots and celery to go in it. I was so focused on what I was doing that when I heard a firm tap on the back door, I squealed in fright and nicked my thumb with the knife.

"Sonofabitch," I cried, grabbing for a paper towel even before walking over to the back door.

It was very early in the morning, just after three, but I wasn't worried it could be one of the paparazzi or even a deranged fan of my dad's at the door. For one, we lived in a secure gated community. No one got in without getting by the four guards that manned the gates at all times.

But when I opened the door, I quickly took two steps back when I saw who stood on the other side. "Go away," I snapped at Braxton.

He crossed his arms over his massive chest, his dark eyes hooded as he glared down at me. "What the hell are you doing answering the door without even asking who it is? It's three in the morning. I could have been anyone here to hurt you. Damn it, Nevaeh! You have no awareness of your own personal safety."

"I knew it wasn't anyone here to hurt me, asshole. I figured it was one of my aunts or uncles checking on us. Or someone from Seller's security, making sure I was okay since the kitchen light was on." Pissed, I started to shut the door in his face, but he caught it before it could close and pushed his way into the house.

His gaze went to the stove where I was cooking, then back to the paper towel I had pressed to my thumb. "What happened?" he growled when he saw the blood staining the paper towel. He reached out to grasp my hand, but I quickly moved away, going to the sink to rinse the small wound.

"You scared me, and I cut myself," I told him over my shoulder.

"Fuck. I'm sorry, Kitten." I felt his heat right behind me a second before he was clutching my arm and lifting my hand to inspect the injury. It was barely anything and it sure as hell wouldn't need stitches, but the way he was looking at it would make anyone think I was about to lose an appendage or something. "Does it hurt?"

"It just stings a little. I'm fine, Brax. Stop fussing. I'll live." Pulling my hand away, I walked over to the drawer where Mom kept a small first aid box. After putting a smear of antibiotic ointment on the cut, I pulled out a bandage.

Braxton took it from me and opened it, then carefully wrapped my thumb. When he was done, he lifted my hand and kissed the bandage. He closed his eyes, and his nostrils flared as he inhaled and exhaled deeply. I wanted to look away, but my eyes reverted to him every time I tried. His handsome face twisted, making him look like he was in agony, and my heart clenched at the sight.

"Why are you here?" I choked out after nearly a full minute had passed.

"I couldn't sleep without you," he murmured, and his eyes finally opened. "I only meant to check the outside of the house to make sure you were safe, but then I saw the kitchen light on and smelled something cooking."

"I'm making homemade chicken noodle soup for Daddy and Uncle Shane," I told him and moved back to the stove and chopping board. I finished cutting up the vegetables and tossed them into the pot with the chicken. Returning the lid to the pot, I set a two-hour timer and turned back to face the man who was making Mom's huge kitchen feel claustrophobic.

"It smells delicious already."

"Thanks," I muttered lamely. Walking over to the coffeepot, I pulled down two mugs from the cabinet above it and filled one before handing it to him and then making a cup for myself. I should have been demanding he leave, but even though my heart was aching and I was pissed as hell at him, part of me didn't want him to go.

He shifted, and I saw him grimace. I knew his leg was hurting him, so I moved to the kitchen table and sat, knowing he wouldn't unless I did first. As expected, he took the seat beside me, and I heard his relieved exhale.

"Did you bring your pain meds?"

"No, but Mia remembered to pack them when she grabbed my things for me." I flinched at the sound of her name, and he muttered a curse. "We really were just trying to protect you, baby."

"By keeping me in the dark about what was going on with you?" Tears filled my eyes, and I tried to blink them back, but they fell anyway. "Do you really have so little respect for me that you don't even want to tell me major things that happen in your life?"

"Fuck, Nevaeh," he said with a groan and reached for my hands. Lifting them, he kissed each palm. "Of course I respect you. I love you."

"I really don't know what to believe anymore. You swore it was all just in your parents' heads and that you would never marry Darcy. You promised no secrets. Then she showed up at the house with an actual wedding invitation, saying you and Mia helped her mom and yours pick it out." I shook my head, causing more tears to spill over my lashes. "I was blindsided, Braxton. I had Mom on the phone, telling me about Daddy. And I still don't remember what she said because I was so focused on Darcy, who was tearing my heart out of my chest. She said…" I sucked in a deep breath. "She said she didn't mind if you kept me. That every guy has a mistress."

He muttered something vicious and cupped my face in both his hands. "Listen to me, baby. Just listen. Yes, Mia and Lyla went with me to my parents' house. My mom was home and there with Darcy's mom, Julia. They were looking at wedding invitations and other shit, and my first instinct was to tell them to pack all of it up and toss it in the trash. But I had to find out if Darcy was pregnant."

Remembering Mia saying Darcy was pregnant hurt all over again. I closed my eyes and tried to pull away from him, but he kept his hands on my cheeks and leaned in closer, brushing his lips over the tip of my nose. "Yes, she is pregnant, but I swear I haven't touched her. We hadn't seen each other in years, baby. That's the God's honest truth. From the day I first set eyes on you, no one else existed for me. No one."

I wanted to believe him, but I couldn't allow myself to trust him. I'd given in easily the last time, and I refused to make the same mistake again.

"I know I broke my promise to you about no secrets, and I'm sorry. But you were so torn up over Drake being sick, and I didn't want to add more stress to you." He pressed his forehead to mine. "Once I knew what was going on with Darcy and how I figured into her plans, I was going to tell you everything, baby, I swear."

Clenching my eyes shut, I sucked in a deep breath and slowly released it. Scooting my chair back, I moved so he wasn't able to touch me and stood. "If you want to stay, you can take the couch. I would say you could have my bed since there is no way I can sleep, but Arella and the others are sound asleep in my room."

"Baby, tell me you believe me," he commanded in a voice raspy with emotion.

"I don't know what to believe right now," I told him honestly. "And even if I did believe you, you broke your promise. How do I know you won't do it again and again? I thought that what we had was special. That you loved me the same way I love you, but you've shown me just how wrong I was."

"No! I'm sorry I broke my promise. So fucking sorry. If I could go back and change it, I would. But I can't." He stood and reached for me, but when I flinched, his face paled and he dropped his hands. "I love you more than I've ever loved anyone, Nevaeh. Baby, please. I need you."

A sad laugh escaped me, and yet another tear spilled down my cheek. "You don't need me, Brax. If nothing else, I do know that much."

"You don't know anything right now," he exploded angrily, frustration and devastation pouring off him in waves. Scrubbing his hands over his scruffy jaw, he walked across the kitchen then jerked around to face me. "This whole thing with your dad has gotten your head turned upside down. You're hurt and pissed, but you're not thinking straight."

"Stop using my dad's illness as an excuse for everything!" I yelled at him. "You fucked up, Braxton. You kept this from me. You broke my heart. None of this has to do with Daddy being sick or having surgery or anything else. It's on you and no one else."

"Baby, we can work this out. Just give me a chance. I'll fix this. P-please, Kitten."

When his voice cracked, my heart shattered a little more. I wanted to hug him, tell him it was all going to be okay, but we both knew that was a lie. It wasn't okay. Nothing between us was now, and it never would be again.

Chapter 21
Braxton

My eyes burned with unshed tears as I watched the love of my life stumble back and then take off running.

Away from me.

Unsteady on my feet, somehow I made it back to the table and slumped into a chair before putting my head in my hands and letting the tears fall.

I was losing her.

She was right. This was all on me. I'd fucked up royally, and now I had no clue how to fix it. But I needed the chance to try. Because I couldn't live without her. I didn't even want to consider the possibility.

The tears kept falling, but I didn't wipe them away. I couldn't even move, frozen in place by the fear that I'd lost the only truly good thing I'd ever gotten to call mine. I sat there for a long time, just crying and trying to come up with a solution to fix what I had broken.

The timer on the stove finally stirred me, and I got up on autopilot to turn off the alarm. Behind me, I heard someone coming into the kitchen at the same time my phone rang. I pulled it from my pocket as I turned to watch Nevaeh cross toward me.

"This is Braxton." I answered the phone without checking to see who it was first.

"Brax." Lyla's strained voice filled my ear, and I immediately went on alert. A look at the digital clock on the stove said it was after five in the morning Pacific time, which meant it was after eight in Virginia.

"Lyla?" I strained to hear anything in the background, worried about my cousin. Then I realized she would have called Howler before me if she were in danger since she knew both Barrick and I were on the West Coast. "What's wrong?"

"The tail you put on Darcy just dropped off a file since Barrick told him you were unavailable. I looked at it… I know I shouldn't have, but I couldn't stop myself. And I kind of wish I hadn't. I can't unsee what I just saw." She was rambling, and that was completely unlike her, so I knew it must be something that had really upset her. "Ah fuck, I wish I could unsee that shit."

I felt Nevaeh's gaze and looked at her. Her face was pale, her blue-gray eyes swollen and red-rimmed, telling me she'd been crying for a while. Yet her brows were lifted, concern on her face for my cousin.

Clenching my free hand into a fist to keep myself from reaching for Nevaeh, I tried to focus on Lyla. "Ly, maybe you should just tell me what you can't unsee, sweetheart. You're kind of rambling right now and not making much sense."

"Yeah, okay." She sucked in a deep breath then released it slowly. "Okay," she said again. "So, the guy tailed Darcy for the past two weeks and finally caught her meeting up with the man I'm assuming is her baby daddy. Ugh. It's so gross, Brax. Like, I seriously want to vomit right now."

"Lyla!" I snapped. "Just fucking tell me."

"She met up with your dad, Braxton. There are pictures, lots and lots of pictures of them in compromising positions—although he's kind of agile for such an old man. Still, gross."

"Wait…" I muttered, trying to keep up with her. "My dad? As in, Darcy is fucking my father?"

"Fucking. Dominating. Making him her bitch. Whatever you want to call it, it looks like that's what is happening in these sick pictures." She made a gagging noise, but I was too stunned to tell her to chill.

Darcy and my father.

Which meant Darcy was pregnant with my little brother or sister.

That was so fucked up.

If Darcy had gotten her way, she could have pretended her lover's child was mine since my dad and I looked similar. We could have the same blood type, share DNA.

And they were both trying to pass it off as mine. Trying to fuck up my life because they'd screwed around and now Darcy was knocked up.

"Brax? You still there?" Lyla's voice finally penetrated my rage-filled fog.

"Yeah, Ly. I'm here." I scrubbed my hands over my face, the lack of sleep and my aching leg finally weighing down on me.

"What do you want me to do with this intel? I can have it overnighted to you, but honestly, you don't want to see your dad being that flexible."

I looked at Nevaeh again, and everything inside me just turned off. I didn't care that my dad was fucking my ex. I didn't care what they did or how they figured this shit out. Let them deal with their own problems, because the only thing that mattered to me was holding on to Nevaeh. "Burn it. Use it as wallpaper. Do whatever the hell you want with it. I don't care anymore, Ly. I'm done with this shit. It's not worth it."

"Worth what?" she asked curiously. "You sound weird. Is everything okay? Fuck, I just realized the time difference. Did I wake you up?"

"No, I was already awake." I blew out an exhausted sigh. "Do what you want with the intel, Lyla. I've got more important things to deal with."

"Are you sure I can do anything with this?"

I grimaced. "Yeah. Whatever you want. Just don't involve me, because I'm done with it all."

"Okay, then. I'll let you get back to whatever it was you were doing at fuck-early in the morning on the West Coast. And if you need anything, Brax, anything at all, just call."

"Thanks. Later, Lyla."

"Bye, cuz."

Dropping the phone on the counter, I leaned back and watched Nevaeh as she took the carrots and chicken from the pot. The chicken was left to cool while she put the carrots in a pan and added a little butter to sauté them with some chopped onion.

"Everything okay with Lyla?" she asked over her shoulder as she turned the burner to low heat before starting to shred the chicken. All while not looking at me once.

"I had a tail on Darcy to find out who her baby's father is," I told her, and I saw her shoulders stiffen. "Turns out, it's my dad."

She turned so suddenly, the forks she was using to shred the chicken fell at her feet. "Shit." I bent to pick them up at the same time she did, our fingers grazing each other. She swallowed hard and snatched them both up before straightening. "I… What? Your dad?"

I was slower to straighten and shrugged. "It makes sense, I guess. Darcy would call me Collins sometimes when we dated. I guess she calls him that too, and her mom just assumed she meant me."

It was more fucked up than I'd first thought when I realized Darcy was pregnant and trying to play her kid off as mine, but I didn't give a single fuck what her plan was now. Nevaeh was more important than dealing with Darcy and my father's freaky relationship.

"That's kind of disgusting," she said, making a face. "I mean, yeah, okay, my parents have a large age gap and all, but it's not big enough that people think he's her father."

"Lyla apparently agrees with you," I told her tiredly.

Nevaeh tossed the forks into the sink and pulled two more from a drawer before glancing at me. "What do you think about all of it? I mean, I know it's got to be weird for you. Finding out the girl you used to have sex with is now doing your father has to be a total mindfuck."

I shook my head. "I haven't given that much thought. I'm more pissed that she was trying to pass my baby brother or sister off as my kid and thought I would just roll over and let her do whatever the hell she wanted."

"Yeah, I can understand that. I mean, you're not exactly a timid or meek kind of guy. If anything, you sometimes border on Neanderthal. A few times over the years, I actually thought I heard you growling 'mine' at people."

"That's because I did," I told her as I stepped up behind her. Inhaling deeply, I breathed in her subtle, sweet floral scent and closed my eyes to savor my favorite smell. "You were always mine, Kitten."

I felt her shiver, and I pressed against her harder. "Brax…" she breathed, but she didn't shy away from my touch when I wrapped my arms around her and pulled her back against my front.

"I love you, Nevaeh. I love you so fucking much. My life is worthless without you in it. Please, baby. Please don't give up on us. Give me another chance."

"Mmm, it smells so good in here," Arella said as she came into the kitchen behind us. "Nev… Oh shit. Sorry, didn't realize you had company."

I turned my head to look at her over my shoulder. "Go back to bed," I told her without releasing her sister.

"Yeah, no." Arella walked to the fridge and pulled out a carafe of orange juice. "I'm wide awake, and I'm not leaving my sister all alone with you when she just spent the last few hours crying her eyes out over your ass."

My heart clenched painfully at the thought of my kitten crying because of me, and I instinctively tightened my arms around Nevaeh, afraid she would pull away from me. "I'm not going to make her cry ever again," I vowed to Arella.

She snorted. "Yeah, sure."

"Arella," Nevaeh said warningly. "Stop."

She grumbled something under her breath and replaced the carafe in the fridge. "You need to get some sleep, Nevi. You look like a fucking ghost right now. Daddy will only worry about you if he sees you like this later."

"I'm fine," she muttered, stepping out of my arms.

"You're not fine. When did you last sleep? I bet it wasn't during this week while you studied your ass off for finals." Arella looked at me to back her up. "Am I right? How much sleep did she get all week?"

She was right. Nevaeh had gotten maybe a few hours of sleep every night that week because she'd been studying hard for her finals. Not that she really needed to. She knew everything her professors tried to teach her already, and I had no doubt she could have easily aced those tests without having studied a single minute during the entire semester. Nevaeh was a perfectionist when it came to her education, something everyone on campus knew. More than one professor had groaned over the last two years when they realized they had her in their classes.

My lack of answer had Arella smirking. "Thought so." The smirk dropped from her face when she faced her sister again. "When you have the veggies sautéed, you take your cute ass upstairs and sleep. There will be no going to the hospital for you if you don't get at least five hours of rest. You will not see Daddy looking like a wraith because I refuse to have you stressing him out."

My kitten's shoulders slumped, and she gave a single nod. "You're right. I don't want to worry him or Mom. They've had enough to deal with lately."

"Good girl." Arella lifted her juice to her lips and took a swallow before walking over and taking the spoon from Nevaeh. "Actually, you go on up to bed. I'll finish the soup. That way, I can take a little credit for it."

Nevaeh gave a small laugh, earning her a wink from her younger sister.

"And, you." Arella pointed the wooden spoon at me. "Go with her. Sleep in my bed." Nevaeh started to protest, but Arella shook her head, waving her out of the room. "Yeah, yeah, yeah. I know. You're pissed at him and blah, blah, blah. Trust me on this, big sis. It might have been from a distance, but I've still been watching you two. We all have. And the way this guy looks at you… That is, beyond a shadow of a doubt, what Mom and Daddy have. Which means I seriously doubt either of you could sleep without the other."

"Not two minutes ago, you were ready to kick his ass. Now you want me to sleep beside him?" Nevaeh huffed angrily.

"You were crying then. And he just promised not to make you cry ever again."

"Which you were all derisive about," she reminded the younger girl.

"I hate when you use words like that. Can't you just say I was being snarky and thought he was full of shit?" Sighing dramatically, she stirred the vegetables still sautéing in the pan on the stove. "The truth is, I believe him. And so should you. Now go upstairs and get some sleep. I'll wake you up when it's time to go back to the hospital."

Not wanting to argue with Arella when I was getting exactly what I wanted, I scooped Nevaeh into my arms and carried her out of the kitchen. I carefully climbed the stairs to the second floor and glanced at her bedroom then at the other closed doors, unsure which was her sister's room.

With a heavy sigh, she directed me to Arella's bedroom, and I kicked the door open. Using my elbow, I turned on the overhead light so I could see where I was going on my way to the bed. Once she was safely in the middle of the mattress, I went back to shut and lock the door before switching off the light. On my way back, I kicked off my shoes and pulled my shirt over my head.

As I dropped down onto the bed beside her, I caught the sound of her soft gasp, and I pulled her into my arms.

"Brax—"

"Sleep," I told her in a gruff voice, pressing my nose to the top of her sweet-smelling head. Closing my eyes, I inhaled slowly and forced all my muscles to relax so I could enjoy this. My sinuses stung with unshed tears, and I prayed this wasn't the last time she let me do this. "Let me hold you. That's all I want right now, Kitten. You can yell at me later. Just please, let me hold you."

Chapter 22
Nevaeh

I didn't think I would sleep with all the noise in my head, but everything seemed to catch up with me all at once. I closed my eyes, letting myself relax against Braxton, telling myself I was just going to lie there and rest, thinking I wouldn't get a single moment of sleep.

The next thing I knew, sunlight was filtering in through the window and Arella was standing over me, gently shaking my shoulder. "Nevi," she whispered. "Hey, if you want to go to the hospital with us, you need to get up."

I frowned up at her for a moment, my brain racing to catch up, then reality flooded back in through the sleep fog, and I jerked upright in bed. The arm that was wrapped around me tightened, and Braxton lifted his head, glancing around, assessing.

"What's wrong?" he growled, his eyes narrowed menacingly as he tried to figure out the danger that had made me rush to sit up.

"I was going to let you sleep since you seemed to need it, but I knew you would wake up and be mad if I just left you." Arella gave me a grim smile. "And Mom has already called saying Daddy is wide awake, up out of bed, and moving around. I figured you would definitely want to go with us to see him."

Pushing my hair back from my face, I nodded and tossed back the covers. "Thanks. Give me fifteen minutes, and I'll be ready."

"Okay. We'll be waiting downstairs for you." She shot a look at Braxton then walked to the door and closed it behind her on her way out.

I started to get up, but Braxton only tightened his hold on me. "Brax—"

"Come here," he commanded. He moved so quickly, I didn't even have time to blink as he rolled onto his back and pulled me down on top of him. He twisted his hand in my hair and brought my head down so he could kiss me.

For a moment, I let him, and I found myself kissing him back. It wasn't a demanding kiss, but one that tried to impress on me how much he cared about me. Swallowing hard, I finally lifted my head and quickly pressed against his chest until he released me.

231

Getting to my feet, I was about to make a run for my bedroom when his voice hit me dead center. "I love you, Nevaeh."

I clenched my eyes closed for a moment, letting his words wash over me for only a second before forcing my feet to move without returning the words that bubbled up and begged to be released.

When I walked downstairs a short while later, Braxton was waiting in the living room with my sisters and Damien. The keys to Mom's vehicle hung from Arella's fingers, but when I went to take them from her, she grinned and shook her head. "Nope. Someone else is driving us."

Humming to herself, she practically bounced out of the living room, leaving the rest of us to follow. Muttering a curse because I already suspected who was driving, I grabbed the tote full of tightly sealed containers of soup and freshly baked French bread that was sitting on the coffee table and exited the house behind my brother.

Sure enough, Jordan was just pulling his vehicle into the driveway. As I turned to close the front door, making sure it was locked, Braxton took the tote from me and then clasped my hand in his.

Looking down at our entwined hands, I was overcome with how perfect my smaller one looked in his much larger one, and my heart broke a little more. As I sucked in a shuddering breath, we moved toward Mom's vehicle together, and he opened the back door for me.

"Morning," Jordan greeted as he accepted the keys from Arella and gave me a grin. "I'd ask how you slept, but you look like you're all kinds of hungover."

I flipped him off and got into the second row with Damien and Braxton since Bliss and Heavenleigh were already taking up the third.

"You wound me, Nevaeh. Truly." With a laugh, he got behind the wheel. "We ready?"

"We're good to go," Braxton told him as he shifted his long legs into a more comfortable position.

Jordan cocked a brow at him as he glanced over his shoulder to back out. "Thought you went home with Mia last night."

"Nevaeh was here," he said, as if that explained everything. From the look on the other man's face, it seemed to do just that, and he gave a single nod before concentrating fully on driving.

Rolling my eyes at the two of them, I shifted away from Braxton as much as the small space would allow and busied myself fixing Damien's unkempt hair. He wanted to let it grow out like Daddy's, but Mom wasn't a big fan of his having long hair and tried to keep it short. But it looked like she was losing that war, and he was as shaggy as ever.

Braxton dropped his arm across the back of the seat, his fingers playing with the ends of the ponytail I'd put my hair up in so I didn't have to wash it. He skimmed them over my shoulder every so often, and I tried to ignore the fact that my skin seemed to burn and tingle where they grazed.

By the time we got to the hospital, I was beyond ready to put some distance between us, and I made sure Damien and my two youngest sisters were between us at all times on the walk inside.

Thankfully, most of the paps had cleared out, making it easier to get into the building. But there were still a few hanging around, trying to get a picture of everyone coming and going so they could sell them to the highest bidder. None of them would get a factual story, though. Aunt Harper's magazine was the only one that would have the exclusive on her husband's and brother-in-law's surgeries.

Despite the less chaotic entrance, Seller's security was still in full force, and Braxton gave many of them nods as we passed.

Arella led the way to the private room Mom had told her Daddy had been moved in to, and as soon as we walked in and I saw Daddy sitting up in a chair next to the window, my knees went weak.

He looked pale, but there was a grin on his face as my siblings and I swarmed him. I let the younger kids hug him first, but before Arella could get her chance, I was throwing my arms around him as carefully as I could and burying my face in his long dark hair, a sob breaking free because I was so damn happy to see him awake.

He wrapped his arms around me gently, patting me on the back with his hands. "It's okay, sweetheart," he murmured softly beside my ear. "Daddy's fine now. I promise."

That only made me cry harder. I was almost sick with relief that he was doing so well after such a major surgery. There could have been any number of complications, but other than looking tired and in a little pain, he seemed in good spirits and healthier than the last time I saw him.

"Good gods," a deep voice said from behind me as the door opened. "What's all the ruckus in here?"

Lifting my head, I watched as Uncle Shane slowly walked into the room. A happy cry left me, and I ran across the spacious private room to throw my arms around him. He groaned, then laughed, and I felt him kiss the top of my head. "Easy, kiddo. I'm a little breakable in spots right now."

"Sorry," I mumbled, easing my grip on him. Lifting my head, I blinked back the tears. "Thank you," I whispered. "Thank you so much. You… You saved him." I buried my face in his chest again. "Thank you."

He gave me a squeeze, and I felt him kiss the top of my head again. "Anytime, sweetheart. Anytime at all."

"Hey, I'm the one who should be getting all the love," Daddy complained, but he was smiling when I left Uncle Shane to walk back over to him. Arella stepped back from hugging him, and I sat on the arm of his chair, needing to be as close as I could get to him.

Braxton offered the tote of food to Mom. "Not sure if they can have this yet, but Nevaeh and Arella made soup."

She gave him a small smile. "Thanks. This will be perfect."

"Ah hell, I am starving," Uncle Shane said, rubbing a hand over his lower abdomen. "Harper was only letting me have broth earlier. That's why I snuck over here in hope Lana would feed me."

"Shouldn't you be in a wheelchair or something, Uncle Shane?" Arella asked him, worry wrinkling her brow.

"Nah. Doc said to move around as much as possible. Hurts to breathe, but walking isn't an issue." He moved closer to Daddy and me. "How are you feeling, brother? You sure as hell look better than you did yesterday, that's no lie."

Daddy nodded. "I feel better than I did. Like you said, it hurts to breathe. But honestly, I haven't felt this good since the car accident."

Hearing that made me breathe a little easier, and I was able to dry my tears as the room slowly filled with other family members. Eventually, Aunt Harper appeared and dragged Uncle Shane back to his own private room, telling him he needed to rest.

His stay in the hospital would be considerably shorter than Daddy's, but he still had a few days to go before he would be released.

When Aunt Emmie showed up with Mia and Barrick, I decided it was time to get some coffee.

Braxton stood when I announced my intention. "I'll come with you."

"No," I told him, keeping my voice cool.

"Kitten," he started, a warning in his tone. "You shouldn't go alone."

"I'll go with you, Nevaeh," Jordan offered, rescuing me, and I quickly latched on to it along with his arm. "Arella, you want something?"

Her brow furrowed when she looked from him to me and down to the way I was holding on to his arm like a lifeline, before shaking her head. I wanted to roll my eyes and yell at her that I would never do any of the things she was obviously thinking, but I clamped my mouth shut.

"Mia?" he asked his best friend.

"N-no thanks," she murmured, but her big green eyes were on me, silently pleading for me to forgive her.

Jordan pulled his arm free and then placed his hand at the small of my back. "Text me if anyone needs anything. We'll be back in a few."

As we walked out the door, I heard Daddy demanding, "Someone better tell me what the hell is going on with her. Right now."

My shoulders slumped because I could only imagine what everyone was saying about me as we left. Beside me, Jordan gave me a pat on the back and pressed the call button for the elevator. "You know, I was kind of jealous of how big your family is. I'm an only child, but I always wanted at least one brother or sister. Then I see how crazy and nosy your family is at times, and that jealousy evaporates like smoke."

"You're part of this crazy family regardless of being an only child," I informed him. "Doesn't matter if you're only Mia's best friend. You're one of us."

He grinned. "Yeah, I'm not going to complain too much about that. It has its perks, being considered family of Emmie Armstrong."

That had me snorting out a laugh as we rode down to the cafeteria in the elevator. "I suppose it does."

We were both quiet until after I'd gotten my cup of coffee and he'd made a cup of tea. I frowned as I watched him make it the exact way I knew my sister loved to drink hers.

"She's half in love with you," I blurted out before I could stop myself, then slapped a hand over my mouth. Fuck, I hated my inability to keep thoughts in my head at times.

Jordan jerked in reaction to my announcement, causing hot tea to slosh over the rim of the cup he was adding honey to. Cursing, he shook out his rapidly reddening hand. "What are you talking about?"

I sighed heavily and dropped my hand. "Arella." There was no use in lying about it. "She looks at you like you hung the moon. And while I know you feed off that kind of adoration from the masses of the female population who fall at your feet with just a flick of those pretty, long lashes of yours, my sister doesn't know the score like they do."

"Arella isn't one of the masses to me," he said, his voice becoming all growly.

"Good. But she's also young. Too young for anything, serious or otherwise. You're free to do whatever you want, with anyone you want. Except her."

He glared at me angrily. "You honestly think I would do something like that? She's my friend, Nevaeh. Like Mia—"

I held up a hand. "I sure as hell hope not. I know about you and Mia."

He cursed viciously. "That was a one-time thing. She was hurting, and things got crazy. It was long before Barrick even came into her life, and it will never happen again."

"I didn't say it would," I told him frustratedly. "I'm just saying you've never had a purely platonic relationship. And considering how my sister feels about you, I can't see you starting with her."

"Okay, first, Mia and I are completely platonic. I didn't think of her that way before we had sex, and I don't think about her that way now. And I don't think of Arella in that way either."

A soft gasp had us both turning to see Arella standing only a few feet away, Braxton right beside her. Tears filled her eyes as she looked at Jordan as if her heart was breaking. "Y-you slept with Mia?" she whispered, her voice cracking.

Jordan's face paled, and he took a step toward her, causing the uncovered tea to slosh him again. But he didn't seem to feel the sting of the heat burning his hand this time. "Arella—"

Her tear-glazed eyes went from him to me. "I really can't believe you, Nevi. Braxton's not the only guy in the world who can wait years for the one they love. There are plenty of other good guys out there just like him. Why did you have to go put your nose in my business?"

"I'm sorry," I tried to apologize. "Arella, I only wanted to—"

"If you say 'protect me,' I'm going to scream. Everyone wants to protect everyone else in this family. Yet they don't know how to keep their damn noses out of everyone else's business and worry about themselves for once. Maybe if they just left things alone, everyone wouldn't be so miserable all the time." With a huff, she turned her glare back to Jordan. "And just for the record, I'm not in love with you. You don't have to worry, because I don't want you like that either."

Turning, she walked away without a single glance back.

Jordan went after her, dropping the cup of tea in the trash on his way out the door. I watched them, feeling guilty for having stuck my foot in it. If I'd kept my mouth shut, my sister wouldn't have been so upset.

Braxton walked over to me. Taking my coffee from my hand, he lifted it to his lips and took a sip. "Your dad wants to talk to you," he said when he handed my cup back to me.

I should have known he would. Not much got by him, apparently not even when he was less than twenty-four hours out of a life-changing surgery.

Chapter 23
Nevaeh

Daddy's room was empty of everyone except him when Braxton opened the door for me a few minutes later. For some reason, I felt nervous as I stepped inside and the door closed behind me. It was just him and me in the huge room, and I wiped my sweat-dampened palms on my jeans as I walked toward him.

He was still sitting in the chair where I'd left him earlier, his jaw tense as he watched me approach.

"Hi, Daddy," I greeted with a nervous smile.

Something softened in his blue-gray eyes when he saw how anxious I was, and he nodded to the chair beside his as I neared. "Sit with me. We need to talk."

I sat on the edge of the chair, turning my body to face him.

"Has anyone ever told you what a fuckup I used to be, Nevaeh?" he asked after a moment.

I blinked at him from behind my glasses. "You could never be a fuckup, Daddy."

His laugh was self-deprecating, and he shook his head, causing his long hair to fall into his face. "Trust me on this, sweetheart. I was the biggest fuckup in history. The day I realized your mom loved me the way I loved her was the same day she left me. That was when I checked myself in to rehab for the first time. Sure, I'd gone plenty of times before, but it was never my choice. Losing her made me open my eyes and realize I was tired of letting my addiction mess up my life."

I frowned at him, still unable to picture him the way he was trying to paint himself. "What did you do to make Mom leave you? I mean… I just can't picture the two of you breaking up. You get upset when you're away from each other for more than a few hours at a time."

His face twisted with pain, but I didn't think it was physical discomfort. And when he spoke, it was choked. "I cheated."

"Stop lying, Daddy," I snapped at him. "You would never do something like that to Mom. Never."

He shook his head. "But I did. Look, I'm not going to fill your head with everything that happened. Most of that is only your mom's and my business. But the truth is, I fucked up, and it cost me seven months with my Angel."

"Why are you telling me this?" I demanded, confused as to why he was revealing something I never would have known about his and Mom'a relationship if he hadn't told me.

"Because I want you to see that even when a man loves a woman as desperately as I love your mom, we can still make mistakes." He reached for my hand and gave it a firm squeeze. "Braxton told me what happened. All of it."

"Daddy—"

He held up the other hand, the one with the IV in the back of it. "I'm not saying what he did wasn't wrong. Honestly, I'm not. I understand why you're upset. I do. Don't think I'm making light of what you're feeling, Nevi. Because even right now, I want to kick his ass for hurting you."

"Then what are you saying?" I muttered.

"What I'm saying is…" He paused and shook his head. "Over the last few years, I've watched that boy. And before my eyes, I saw what he feels for you blossom into something lasting. After a while, I stopped worrying so much about you being so far away from us because I knew Braxton would move heaven and earth to keep you safe and happy. He loves you. And don't you lie and say you don't love him just as much."

"I wasn't going to lie. Yes, I love him. I don't want to, but I do." Which was why my heart hurt so much.

"You have to know that he isn't going to marry this Darcy chick," he chided. "You know him better than that. He loves you too much to even look at another person, least of all marry someone else."

"I know," I whispered, because I did know. It wasn't so much that I thought Braxton would actually marry Darcy. It was that he kept everything from me. That he broke his promise.

"Then why—"

"Why are you on his side?" I cried. "He's the one who broke my heart. Not the other way around. Braxton lied to me. He kept all of this to himself after he promised we wouldn't have secrets from each other."

"Because I've been in his shoes." His voice rose as he spoke. "I lost the woman I love because I was dumb and drunk, and I will regret it until my dying day. And I don't want you or him to go through that hell, Nevaeh. He made a mistake, and he regrets it."

"But how am I supposed to trust him not to break every other promise he makes to me?" I asked desperately, twin tears spilling down my cheeks. "How do I put my trust and faith in him not to break my heart again and again?"

Daddy's brows rose. "How many has he broken before now?"

"What?"

He leaned forward and grimaced in pain, but he cupped my chin and tilted it up so he was looking into my eyes. "How many promises has he broken before now?"

That gave me pause, and I quickly thought back through any promises Braxton might have made in the past. "He… He never made me any promises before this one."

"Bullshit."

"Daddy, I swear, he never made me any other promises. This was the first."

"You're wrong, sweetheart. He's made you and me plenty. Keeping you safe was the first one he ever made me. Not once has he broken that. And he might not have made you any promises aloud, but trust me when I say his eyes have made you plenty." He gently released me and sat back, groaning in discomfort. "I think you owe it to yourself to give him one more chance, Nevi. Just one more. And if he fucks up again, if he breaks your heart even once more, then I'll kill him."

A choked laugh escaped me, because his voice was suddenly dripping with venom and menace. "Daddy, you know I love you, right?"

He took hold of my hand again, giving it a squeeze. "You couldn't possibly love me as much as I love you, Nevaeh Joy. But yeah, I know you love me."

***

When I opened the door, I wasn't surprised Braxton was standing there waiting. He leaned back against the wall, his face blank as he gazed straight ahead without seeing anything. As the door closed behind me, he blinked and focused on me, life returning to his handsome face as he straightened.

"Are you hungry?"

Eating wasn't exactly the first thing on my mind, but at the mention of food, my stomach growled hungrily, making his lips tip up with amusement.

"I'll take that as a yes. Let's go." He took my hand without asking and guided me toward the elevators.

"I really don't think I can stomach cafeteria food right now," I told him as he hit the button for the first floor, where the cafeteria was.

"I would never make you eat hospital food, Kitten." The doors opened again, and we walked off, my hand securely in his.

Outside, there was a small line of cabs, and we walked up to the first one. He got in first, something he always did when we went anywhere in a cab or Uber. The one time I'd tried to get in before him, he'd growled at me how dangerous it was. It had melted me, and instead of rolling my eyes at him in annoyance, I'd promised never to do it again.

Leaning forward, he told the driver where to take us then sat back. I shifted on the seat, unsure what to say. But when I finally opened my mouth to speak, he lowered his head and brushed a kiss over my lips. "Don't," he murmured. "Just let me have a little longer with you. One more meal. Please. That's all I'm asking."

Lifting my hand, he pressed it to his chest as he leaned back, and I quickly snapped my mouth shut.

The driver stopped in front of one of my favorite restaurants, a little Italian place that looked like a hole-in-the-wall but served the best food. My parents used to take us there when I was younger, and they would tell us the story of how they had dinner there before they even started dating. It was the same story every time, one that wasn't even very romantic given that Mom was only seventeen at the time and Uncle Shane was a third wheel. But I loved that damn story, and the food was amazing.

There was no way Braxton had known about this place on his own. I'd never told him about it. Which meant Mom must have.

As we entered, a hostess came out from behind the podium with a welcoming smile on her face. "Table for two?"

Braxton nodded, my hand still pressed to his chest. I could feel how hard his heart was pounding, and it worried me that he was going to have a heart attack if he didn't calm it down soon.

The hostess beamed at him and picked up two menus, leading the way to a quiet booth in the back.

With the promise of sending someone to take our order quickly, she left us alone.

I glanced down at the booth, and Braxton finally eased his hold on my hand so I could take a seat. But instead of sitting across from me, he nudged me to scoot over and took the place beside me.

As soon as he was seated, he retook my hand. Lifting it to his lips, he kissed my knuckles and then pressed it back over his heart. The quiet between us was deafening, and I'd just opened my mouth to ask him if he was okay when the waitress arrived to take our drink order and ask if we would like an appetizer.

"Just water," I told her with a tiny smile, and then Braxton ordered the same and an appetizer sampler.

Moments later, we were alone again, and I couldn't stand the silence that shrouded us in return. "Braxton—"

"I know your dad probably told you to cut your losses and move back here. I'll accept that and won't make things more difficult for you, Kitten. Just…" He released a heavy sigh, and I watched as a single tear fell from his dark eyes. "Just let me have one more hour with you."

I pinched my brows together. "Why would you think Daddy would say that?"

"I told him everything. If it were my daughter, I would be telling her to dump the douchebag, and then I'd kill the bastard." His shoulders lifted in a shrug, and my heart twisted with love for him when another tear dripped off the end of his lashes.

I wiped it away with the thumb of my free hand, then leaned in to kiss his scruff-covered jaw. "Good thing you aren't Daddy, then. Because that would have been a stupid thing to tell our daughter."

He jerked in reaction to my words. "What?"

I shook my head at the confusion in his tear-glazed eyes. "Daddy didn't tell me to dump you, but he did mention killing you if you break my heart again."

"As he should," he said gruffly.

"What he said was that I should give you one more chance, because you have never once broken a promise before." I bit my lip, thinking just how smart my dad was because he was right. About everything. "That was what hurt the most, Brax. Not so much Darcy, because she is just an attention-seeking bitch. And not the wedding, because I knew you would never actually do something like that to me. But when you kept it all from me… That was what broke me."

"Baby." He cupped my face and pressed his forehead to mine. "I'm sorry. It's never going to happen again. I never meant to hurt you. It's killing me that I did. Causing you pain causes me pain."

"You better not. I don't think I could stop my dad from killing you if you do." I'd meant to tease him, but his face was serious when he stroked his thumb from the corner of my eye down my cheek.

"If I so much as make a single tear fall from these beautiful eyes again, I'll let him do his worst," he vowed. "I love you more than life, Kitten. Because you *are* my life."

The waitress cleared her throat to announce her arrival as she placed our glasses of water on the table in front of Braxton. "Er, sorry. Um, are you two ready to order?"

I swallowed a laugh at the scowl on Braxton's face and quickly saved the girl from him. "Salad starter for both of us. Dressing on the side. Chicken parm for me, and he will have the lasagna. And please keep the breadsticks coming."

She let out a relieved breath as she scribbled everything down, promised the appetizers would be out shortly, and booked it back to the kitchen.

Grinning up at Braxton, I kissed his chin. "I'm assuming Mom told you this is one of my favorite restaurants."

"She might have said if I wanted back in your good graces, this was the right place to start," he confirmed. But then his hands were tangling in my hair, and he was angling my head back so he could kiss me hungrily.

My mouth felt tender and swollen when he finally lifted his head. "I love you so fucking much."

Gasping for breath, I pulled his head back down to mine. "I love you too."

Chapter 24
Braxton

Still kissing Nevaeh's lips, I scanned the keycard over the hotel room door lock and heard the click before pushing the thing open. Her giggle was sexy as fuck as I ravished her mouth while steering us into the room and trying to avoid the obstacles blocking the direct path to the bed.

After eating, she'd whispered how hot she imagined make-up sex would be, while caressing her fingers up the inside of my thigh. Two seconds later, I had an Uber ordered and we were making out. I barely remembered the ride to the five-star hotel or even checking in, because she tried her hardest to distract me even as I was handing over my credit card—and she succeeded beautifully.

Finally, my thigh hit the edge of the bed, and I tumbled backward, taking her with me. She fell across my chest, kissing my neck while her fingers made quick work of my belt and the top snap of my jeans.

"Missed you so fucking much," I told her as I tugged her shirt up over her head and tossed it across the room, then filled my hands with her luscious tits.

"We weren't even apart for a day," she reminded me breathlessly.

"I miss you every minute you're not beside me," I told her honestly.

"Braxton," she choked out, her chin trembling.

"No," I growled and rolled her beneath me. "No tears."

She gasped, the sound going straight to my cock, and shook her head. "Happy tears, I swear."

"Don't care. No tears. I'll lose my mind." Bending, I attacked her mouth, kissing her until I was sure she wouldn't cry. When I finally released her, she was clinging to me and mewling like the kitten she was.

It took me a matter of seconds to get her naked beneath me, and I moved even faster to shed my own clothes. Then I was sliding deep into her tight, wet heat and we were both groaning in relief. Finally, we were one again, and I never wanted to leave the sweet haven of her pussy.

It was hours before either of us was sated or exhausted. Gasping for breath, she pressed her sweat-dampened brow against my chest, kissing right over my heart. Content, I stroked my fingers down her back, thanking every deity I could think of that I hadn't lost my kitten.

But there was one thing I was still curious about.

"Why did your dad tell you to give me another chance?" I asked her.

Nevaeh lifted her head, a sleepy look in her eyes. "He said he didn't want either of us to go through the hell he went through with Mom. They broke up for like seven months once, and he said it was the worst time of his life."

"Why did they break up?" I couldn't imagine Drake without Lana or her without him. The very idea of it felt like some alien, alternate universe.

Her eyes darkened. "That's his story to tell," she said after a slight hesitation. "It really isn't my past to share. But he regrets it more than anything he's ever done. And according to him, he fucked up a lot."

"Whatever happened with them, I'm grateful to him for convincing you to give me another chance." I cupped her sweet ass in each of my hands, giving both globes a firm squeeze. "But do you think you can forgive Mia too?"

Nevaeh snorted and propped her chin up on her hand. "You sweet, lonely only child."

My brows furrowed at that. "What does that mean? Is it a yes? Because I really don't know."

Laughing, she rolled onto her back and then sat up. Once she was standing, she walked over to where I'd tossed her jeans earlier and found her phone. I sat up, appreciating her nakedness and the delicious view of her ripe ass as she bent over.

Pulling out her phone, she waved it at me. "Texts from Mia. And one from Arella." She frowned. "Fuck, she's still mad at me." Then with a shrug, she walked back to the bed and crawled under the covers with me.

"Nevaeh," I growled when she started texting. "About Mia."

"Braxton," she laughed, barely looking at me as she texted rapidly. "I have three sisters and a shitload of female cousins—both honorary and by blood—with whom I fight regularly. It lasts like a day most times, a week tops, and then we're all good again."

"I fight with Barrick and Lyla too, but I don't toss things like 'we're no longer family' at them." I tapped her on the nose with my index finger, making her scrunch it up. In the two years I'd known her and Mia, they had never fought, but that didn't mean they hadn't in the past. Still, I didn't like it when either of them was upset. "And you threw that at Mia a shit-ton, baby. I love you so fucking much, but you were killing me with that crap you tossed at her."

She rolled her eyes. "It's not the first time I've thrown that out at one of my cousins, or even one of my sisters. Trust me on this. Mia and I are cool." To prove it, she shoved the screen of her phone into my face. "See? We're currently talking baby names."

And they fucking were. Mia had texted Nevaeh a list of names she liked for both boys and girls, and Nevaeh had already sent back her top five picks from each. Groaning, I took the phone from her and tossed it to the end of the bed. "Come here, Kitten."

Giggling, she shifted away from me. "No way. As it is, I'm going to be walking funny for the next few days. You fucked me so hard, I can still feel you."

"My poor little baby," I murmured, pinning her beneath me. "Don't worry. I'll kiss it all better."

The moan that left her as I licked her swollen clit, however, sounded anything but pained. She fisted her hands in my hair, holding me to her pussy as I sucked her tenderly until she was begging me to fuck her again.

Epilogue
Nevaeh

Pulling off my cap, I carefully made my way through the masses of other excited college graduates who were celebrating with their friends and family. I already knew where all of mine were, and I was working my way to them so the others in my graduating class weren't trampled in the stampede.

I heard my sisters yelling my name even before I'd taken a few steps, and I lifted my hand to wave at them even though I couldn't see them yet.

Before I could reach them, however, I was swept off my feet and twirled around. I wrapped my legs around Braxton's waist, my fingers thrusting into his hair as I kissed him. A growl left him, making me grin as I lifted my head just enough to rub my nose against his.

"Congratulations, Miss Top of Her Class" he said with a smug grin on his sinfully handsome face. "Your speech kicked ass."

"Well, I had this hot Marine vet help me write it, so I can't take all the credit." I kissed him again then unwrapped my legs from around his waist, but he didn't release me. His hands gripped my ass and held me in place.

Laughing, I shook my head at him. "My dad loves you, but he might murder you on the spot if he sees this hard-on I currently feel pulsing against my core, Brax."

"Hold on," he said and slowly set me on my feet.

"Nevaeh!" I heard Bliss shouting somewhere not too far away.

"Nevi!" Arella yelled my name.

But Braxton suddenly had my full attention as he cupped the back of my head in one hand and brushed his lips softly over mine in a kiss that was so gentle, it brought tears to my eyes. When he lifted his head only moments later, I had to suck in a fortifying breath.

"I love you," he rasped. "So fucking much. And before you say anything about your dad or those damn annoying sisters of yours trying to get you to look at them, know that I already told Drake what I'm about to do and got his full support to do it."

I lifted my brows at the last part, but before I could say anything, he was suddenly on his knees in front of me. With my left hand secure in his right, he pulled something out of his suit pants pocket and opened a tiny ring box.

I couldn't breathe, couldn't tear my eyes away from his even to look at what was in the box. There were hope and fear in his dark eyes, and even though I saw his lips moving, I couldn't hear a single word he said because my brain was screaming, *"He's really fucking doing it. He's really fucking doing it,"* on repeat over and over again.

Then he was just staring at me, the fear completely smothering the hope in those eyes I loved so much. Tears filled them, and I suddenly realized I hadn't answered him yet.

"Yes!" I squealed and threw my arms around his neck. The momentum sent us both crashing to the ground, him beneath me, and the ring box in his hand fell beside us. "Yes, Brax. I'll marry you. Of course I will."

A tear was already spilling over his lashes, and I quickly kissed it away, then every inch of his face. "I love you. I love you so much. Please, can we get married tomorrow?"

His happy laugh vibrated into my chest. "Fuck," he groaned. "You scared the living hell out of me just now. I thought you weren't going to say yes."

"Dude." I heard Daddy's voice from somewhere nearby and looked up to find him and Mom walking toward us, hand in hand. "I knew she would get you on your knees, but I wasn't expecting you to be on your back quite this soon."

I jumped up off the man I loved and threw myself into Daddy's arms. In the last five months, he'd only gotten healthier. And every time Braxton and I went to California to visit with them, I saw the changes. Daddy was leaner now, but a good lean, and there was a new glow to his skin. It gave me hope that he was going to be with us for a long, long time to come.

But I missed my family, something Braxton knew and accepted. Which was why he'd been the one to suggest we find a place to rent close to my parents while I went to grad school there.

"Hold up, Kitten." Braxton pulled me away from my dad. Taking my left hand back in his, he slid the ring onto my finger, and I finally looked down at it.

Mom gasped appreciatively as we both admired the huge pear-shaped diamond, surrounded by a dozen smaller ones. The sunlight overhead hit the ring, making it sparkle prettily, and I flexed my fingers, loving the effect.

Looking up at Brax, I swallowed the tears that were trying to block my throat. "I really do want to marry you tomorrow."

"Wait!" Mom shouted. "You are not getting married tomorrow. I've been thinking of this ever since your last visit when Brax asked your dad if he could marry you."

"Angel," Daddy said with mock sternness. "The girl wants a quick wedding."

"But...all those pretty wedding dresses I've been looking at." She pouted at him then turned it on me. "Nevi, come on. I swear I won't go crazy with this thing. Something small. Give me two months. Three, tops. We'll make this wedding so beautiful, and your dad can walk you down the aisle. And—"

Braxton wrapped his arms around me from behind and kissed my neck. "Let her have her way, Kitten. She can plan the whole thing while you and I go house hunting."

"House hunting?" Daddy repeated, his eyes sparkling with more than a little hope of his own. "Where exactly will you be looking at houses?"

"Santa Monica?" I murmured with a sly grin.

"Fuck yeah!" Daddy bellowed and swung me up into his arms. "Emmie!" He yelled, and like magic, my aunt materialized out of the crowd behind us. "Em, find my girl a house. Cost means nothing."

"Wait, wait!" I tried to argue. "Daddy, you don't have to buy me a house. I want to be closer to you and Mom, but that's too much."

"Braxton," Dad said, his tone serious. "I changed my mind. You can only marry her if she lets me buy her a house."

His face paled, but he quickly nodded. "Yes, sir. I'll take care of it, sir."

"What?" I gaped from one man to the other. "No! We are not letting him buy us a house. Mom, tell him."

But Mom lifted her hands in mock surrender. "Sorry, sweetheart, no can do. Daddy's already made up his mind." Then she squealed and threw her arms around me, jumping up and down like she was a teenager. "A wedding, house hunting, and getting my baby closer! This is better than Christmas."

Seeing how happy she and Daddy were, I finally gave up arguing and let them have their way.

Braxton kissed my shoulder as we watched my parents talk through everything animatedly with Aunt Emmie, who was furiously typing all the details into her phone. "Think they would notice if we disappeared for a few hours?"

I leaned back into him. "Doubtful."

"Good. Because I need to make love to you with nothing on but that ring." Swinging me up into his arms, he carried me off. And not a single one of them noticed.

Needing Nevaeh

Coming Next

Sweet Agony
Angels Halo MC Next Gen
Book 2

Savoring Mila
Angels Halo MC Next Gen & Rockers' Legacy (Crossover)
Book 3

Loving Violet
Rockers' Legacy
Book 4

Surviving His Scars
Angels Halo MC Next Gen
Book 4